CW00688435

Stan Bubbles, Evil Overlord M.D.

Stan Bubbles Trilogy, Volume 1

Kim Adkins

Published by Iron Umbrella Publishing, 2024.

This is a work of fiction. Similarities to real people, places, or events are entirely coincidental.

STAN BUBBLES, EVIL OVERLORD M.D.

First edition. April 2, 2024.

ISBN: 979-8224383092

Written by Kim Adkins.

To those who said I couldn't.

I did.

ONE

No. I do not use my real name when I work. "But kids would love it! It's Doctor Bubbles!" Yea... You don't live where I do.

My family has ruled over this tropical country for at least ten generations. Oh, and every single one of them has been pure evil.

I'm not talking scheming and kiniving to take the throne from each other, I'm talking about boiling would be heros alive and keeping the reign through fear and owning most of the money our little country of Farysha on the continent Asura has. THAT sort of evil.

Of course that also means that they never split up the fortune between their kids, and being the youngest and thirteenth child I had no hopes of gaining anything from my wealthy parents. So, I estranged myself and studied Medicine and Magical Application at the Archipelago University. After years of hard work I graduated youngest of my class as Stan Bubbles, M.D. and quickly found I could NOT get a job anywhere.

Which means a little bit of that Magical Application to duplicate and alter I.D.s and Certifications and within the week I got my job! So far no one has discovered my true identity, and I have been working here for a good decade now, they're planning a secret party for me next week that they think I have no clue about. It's cute. Well, I should say they're planning a party for Doctor Stan Kadhäb.

I had just locked up my office at Hykur Memorial for the night after a long conversation with a giggling nurse, Hope, who insisted on asking repeatedly how long I had been here when my cell phone rang.

"Doctor Kadhäb." I answered.

1

"It's Bubbles, stop using that fake name." My older brother scolded from the other end. Harry Bubbles, he who is set to inherit the title of Lord Bubbles. Where I had the brains of the family, he was blessed with raw talent for the magical arts. Or, rather, for magically setting things on fire.

"You know if I start using my actual name I'll be fired within the hour..." I mumbled. He didn't hear me and continued as if I said nothing.

"Lil bro, you coming to the family outing next week?" He asked me.

"No, I have other plans."

"On a Thursday?"

The party was on Wednesday at work, but that doesn't mean I had to tell Harry the truth. I simply did not want to be around the family that only cared on the surface for the youngest child, or rather only cared for the eldest three.

"Yes, on a Thursday." I growled. "I'm a doctor. I have patients to see." Not a lie exactly, but not the reason I didn't want to go.

"Well, then call in sick." Harry suggested. "There's gotta be back-ups."

"Out of sick days. That lockdown six months ago for a virus that I never actually had any patients come in with took it all for mandatory stay at home time."

My brother chuckled. "Yea, that's a fun tactic..." He muttered to himself. "Anyway, you have a degree in magic, just make an illusionary clone of yourself to go to work."

"When you do that and visit me in double and have your clone passably act like you, then I'll try the spell." The challenge was put out there, he'd try to meet it later. If he ever turned down a challenge I'd worry that he was on his deathbed.

"I'll do that one day." I could hear the snark in his voice. "But for now, Thursday, all day, the family Yacht."

I sighed as I stopped by my bike. On the wall the bike rack was facing someone had spray painted "No Bubbles are Good Bubbles" with little bubbles all around it being popped by an angry dragon. Whoever had done this would have been caught on camera and executed by now. Must be fresh though, as the cleaning crew hadn't shown up to wash it off yet. I let Harry stew in silence as I leaned down and grabbed the magi-lock with my bare hand, allowing the device to scan my aura and unlock.

"All I can promise is that I will try to show up, Harry." I pulled the covered chains from the spokes of the tire and from around the frame. "I can't just not show up to work, some of us have to make an effort to make a living. And besides, the harbor is a long way to bike from my apartment."

"You still *bike* to work?" The scorn in his voice was thick as butter. "Just buy a car, or I'll get you one for your birthday."

"Then convince father to give me a company credit card for gas while your at it."

"Ha!" He laughed heartily, "As if father would do such a thing. I don't even have a company card!"

"Does Jasmine even have one yet?"

"Doubt it."

I sighed and shook my head, looking around as I heard some people approaching, talking loudly about how they hated a particular, company issued soap. "Sorry I gotta cut this short, but I gotta get home to my cat. Talk to you later?"

"Yea, I'll call you tomorrow or something." Harry offered. We both knew he wouldn't, but at least we were both being polite. "Take care lil bro."

"You too, Harry."

And with that, the phone went silent. There was an odd, silent thrum in the air as the two cleaners approached and I slid my phone into my pocket. I set my briefcase on the little rack behind my seat and used the lock to hold it in place.

"Do we know you?" One of the cleaners asked as they walked up to me. "You didn't do this, did you?"

I chuckled. "No and no. I just work here, you probably saw me if you've come in for an emergency."

"A doctor," the second, shorter cleaner scoffed, "who rides a bike instead of drives a car?"

I rolled my eyes as I sat on my bike. "Yea, I know. Hard to believe a doctor would daaare take a healthy choice."

The two glared at me. I just shrugged. "You're the ones walking to a worksite. Government cleaners are stationed further than my home, yet you're mocking me for biking." The glares grew deeper. I chuckled and turned my back to them. "Ta ta."

I could feel their scowls at my back as I rolled up the slope towards my apartment building. The streets were dim with the setting sun behind my back casting a red glare on the glass panes of the storefronts. Here and there people of different races from humans to Elves, Orcs, and even a couple Gnomes were hurrying about, trying to finish their errands or close up shops before curfew hit in just over an hour when the sun fully set.

The apartment complex was a series of five story tall buildings surrounding a large oasis. The gate guard, a pale Elf with golden eyes, nodded at me as I approached and hit a button, causing the iron gate to swing inward, creaking on its' hinges. He leaned back in his chair as I passed, pulling out a magazine to page through as he sat at his post.

The oasis in the center of the tall buildings had a pool on one side, a hot tub nearby for parents that wanted to relax as their children splashed away. Next to that was a small, fenced dog park. The rest of the area, about a whole acre, was wooded with trails, picnic spots, and tall trees beaming with bright flowers and singing birds. It was a way to bring the nature into the city, though few parks like this existed elsewhere. Hykur was not designed with nature and art in mind, though some architects knew the importance of both subjects.

I found my heart missing the colors and spires of Archipelago University, a city in and of itself, as I rolled my bike up to a set of double doors. I pressed a button on my key ring and the doors opened, allowing me to walk the bike to the elevators where a stocky Dwarf waited.

We nodded at each other as we waited for the lights to show to ground level. No one actually lived on this floor, it was just garages. And no, I'm not keeping my bike in my garage. Theft is still an issue in this city and belongings are just safer when they're on you. Finally the door opened up, and we stepped in, me and my bike before the Dwarf. He got off at the next floor, I waited to the top with no one else jumping in to listen to the horrible music with me. Maybe I should make a call one day and get the music to be changed... Maybe I should call Harry back and talk to him more.... There were many calls I should probably make to be honest.

The doors opened to the bland hall, simple wooden doors lining the walls. My footsteps echoed on the false wood floors, installed for the feel of luxury. Each doorknob in this complex had no locks, rather the knob was the lock in-tuned to the residents aura in much the same way my bike lock works. Wrong person tries to enter and will find the knob as slippery as if it were covered in slime and unable to open. The right person can enter without an issue, and without needing keys. The only keys I had where to the hospital and my office. Heck, the building itself opened with a button, not an actual key.

Finally, I reached the end of the hall to my apartment, number five-hundred and thirteen. I felt the soft tingle of the aura reading magic as I let myself in, awkwardly holding the door open as I pulled my bike inside. I kicked the stand down and left the bike near the door, keys and briefcase still hooked to the back platform. I won't need them until the morning.

My cat, Sir Snowball, a large, white fluffy thing with the mean streak of a fluffy cloud, came up and rubbed on my legs, purring heartily at my return. I scratched at his soft head for a moment, glancing over at his dishes in the kitchen to make sure they were full before I straightened and took in the rest of my place. Sir Snowball made his way back to his stand to continue the nap I am certain I woke him from.

My apartment is one of the fancier options I had to chose from. Two bedrooms, one of which serves as my in home office for when I have to take care of meetings or virtually meet with patients, a decent sized kitchen with a wood paneled breakfast or dining nook, and a living room with a large window overlooking the fake forest below. Everything was sparsely furnished, and my real certificates hung in my office, far enough back from my camera so that no one can read my name on them.

I rummaged through my fridge for anything I could toss in the microwave and heat up, or not, if possible. Finding pizza I chose to just grab the platter and sit in my recliner, turning on the television as I did so. Nonchalantly, I flipped through the channels. Propaganda mostly, media all controlled by my father but each claim that they're owned by different political views. Childrens cartoons, blue dogs that talk, cats that talk, magical wishes, the lightheartedness that children prefer.

After about ten minutes of doing nothing but watching two seconds of a channel and going to another I turned it off and finished my pizza in the light of the setting sun. I pulled out my phone and placed it on the end table besides me, staring at it.

I should call Harry back.... I thought. *Or any of my siblings. Maybe Father, it is his birthday next week.* My eyes just hovered on the phone, my fingers not moving, my hands staying locked to the pizza they held. I set the pizza down on the platter and stood up, stretching.

Maybe I'll just go to bed. I decided. I took the platter back, not even bothering to wrap it up first. I stopped before my office. *Ugh, emails.....* And walked in.

The facial recognition software signed me in as soon as I took my seat. Three different screens came to life, lightening the otherwise dark room. My keyboard lit up in a rainbow of colors and my mouse shown a deep red at the contours. Most of the emails were forwarded to either my spam folder, or to the hospital secretary. A few subscription services reminding me that the auto-renewal was coming up and asking if I still wanted whatever it was. Magazines for the most part that I use in my waiting room.

An hour of sorting through everything and I walked out of the room, the lights shutting off automatically behind me as the software no longer was able to see my face. I stood outside of the room, debating on what to do next. Again, calling some of my family came to mind. I walked over to my phone and checked it for messages, to see if any of them tried to reach out to me first.

Just the call from Harry, nothing else for weeks from any of them. No calls, no texts, nothing. I set the phone down with a defeated sigh. *If none of them want to make an effort, then why should I?*

Not sure what else to do, I wandered into my bedroom. The lights, sensing movement but with no other light source having the curtains to the window being closed, slowly came to life. Having an odd enjoyment of what many refer to as "the Olden Times" where there was no electricity, I had swapped out the bulbs for some that flickered like candles, casting the wood furnished room with a supple, orange light. This was the only room that had anything on the walls, tapestries depicting unicorns and dragons, one of which was legitimately almost a millennia old and any museum would have paid a pretty price for, hung between the lamp sconces.

Thick, plush carpets matched the ornate patterns. Gold and silver threads woven in sparkled in the flickering light, casting a grand appearance to the whole scene. A tall bookshelf filled with tomes as old as the tapestry and reproductions of which I actually would handle took up one wall. A low dresser with a large mirror, again framed by the sconces, sat on the wall with the door. Opposite, a barn door hung on a rod, hiding the closet which was only about half full.

The bed itself stood center of the room, pushed against the wall, a thin, covered, window just above the headboard. A thick, velvet comforter shimmered with golden embroidered flourishes, catching the light from every angle and shining brighter than the carpets. Bright, white pillows popped against the red fabrics, a matching bench for balance stood at the foot of the bed.

This was a room that no one besides myself and Sir Snowball entered. When I had guests they'd sleep in my office, and this door stayed shut. It was the only place I allowed myself a small bit of pride.

I sat on the bench and glanced at my reflection in the mirror as I pulled out some silken pajamas. I didn't look like my father, probably the one aspect that has kept others from realizing my true identity. My eyes were bright blue, almost the color of sea ice, beneath a dark black brow. Matching black hair was cut short, and no beard or mustache marred my pale skin, made a few shades darker by the lighting around me. One could call my sharp features handsome, and I have seen quite a few women glance my way when they thought I wasn't looking. But alas, unless I went through the process to legally change my name I could never wed, and even if I tried the process my Father would simply deny it. That was just the sort of man he was.

I shook my head from such thoughts, and pulled on the pajamas, stretching as I stood. I buttoned the ivory buttons as I walked to the side of the bed.

Once again my mind trailed to calling my family. I just couldn't shake the odd feeling in my gut.

"Lights, off." I muttered, climbing into the tall bed. Darkness consumed the room. Relaxing I decided to give things a few days. Maybe I should try to go to the party on Thursday. It was my Fathers birthday after all....

TWO

The next few days were as inconsiderable as they get. Patients came and left. A couple broken bones that needed setting and casts. Stitches here and there. A lady that I suggested go to a shelter instead of to the obviously abusive home she lived in, proven by the bruises along her arms and sides that he saw during her visit. She had come in complaining of stomach pain, nothing appeared wrong save the too many bruises. Though she tried hiding the black eye with make-up and succeeded fairly well. I had also suggested changing professions to go into the beauty lines.

I hoped she'd listen and not go home as I closed the door after myself, folder in hand.

"Hope," I said to the pale skinned Elf sitting at the back desk. Her eyes shone a deep, dark violet and her golden hair was tied back with a matching purple bow. "please make sure this kind lady gets the archangel prescription if she wants such." Our code for shelter information, and to potentially alert authorities if desired. Not that they would do much, but something is better than nothing.

"On it, Doctor." Hope said, spinning in her chair, pushing off with one long leg to the filing cabinet wall behind the arch of a desk. Gracefully, like a dancer, she stopped her motion, put the folder I handed her into one cabinet and pulled a bundle of papers from another.

"Thank you Hope." I turned to another lady, a small Sprite of bright colors, ticking away information on the computer. "Who's next?"

She nodded in my direction and poked a few of the keys with long fingers tipped with oranges and greens. A moment later she spoke up in a high pitched voice. "One Gnome walk-in, then that's it for the day unless you wanted another walk-in."

"Nah, I'm good." I waved my hand. "Thank you, Frayda. What's the issue with the Gnome?"

She clicked away more at the keyboard. "Looks like an illness, Gem-Bumps, he claims."

"Just in case it is can you prep a prescription for Ybuprogem?" I took the files for the Gnome from the holder. Romeo Scarletcap, claims of itchiness, fatigue, and painful lumps sprouting bright red gems. "Room seven?"

Frayda nodded. "Looks legit, prescription should be ready for pick-up by the time you're through."

"Thank you, nurses." I said, giving the slight Frayda a squeeze on the shoulder and a nod to Hope now handing a packet of papers to the lady I had just seen to as she meekly tried to slip by. "You take care of yourself, ma'am." I added as she looked in my direction.

"I'll try." She muttered meekly.

I smiled warmly as she walked away. "Hope, in a few days can you do a follow up call on her?"

"Of course, Doc." The young Elf smiled. She had just finished all her training a year ago. Her smile was always contagious.

I smiled back. "Off to see Mister Scarletcap about some gemstones." I wiggled the folder as I walked around the desk and down the hall to room number seven.

I knocked on the door to let the Gnome I was there. "Come in."

"Mister Scarletcap?" I asked, looking over the folder even though I already had done so. I find it sets the patients mind at ease seeing such a thing as a first impression.

I looked up as he affirmed his identity. The Gnome was about three feet tall, his red cap was sitting next to him, adorned with hand embroidered swirls. He was balding, though long white hair and a rather impressive beard would give the appearance of a full head once his hat was put in place. What looked like rubies or garnets were scattered across his skin, embedded in angry looking welts. His small eyes were dark and glazed, guessing he was on some sort of medication. I scanned his pages for the blood test: positive Gem-Bumps, positive opium, positive.... Venom?

"Gem-Bumps, I see." I glanced up from the papers as I sat down at the desk, the computer automatically logging me in. The Gnome nodded, slowly.

"On any painkillers?" He shook his head no.

I sighed, and set the folders down on the desk. "Won't do to lie to me, Mister Scarletcap. Between the blood test and your glazed eyes I know you're on something." I held my hands out in a friendly manner. "Please be honest here. I would hate to misdiagnose you."

Very slowly, something not normal for Gnomes, he turned to look at me and nodded.

Just a touch faster than the Gnome moved I shook my head. "Look, I know you can talk, and that Gnomes generally dislike humans. But you came to me. You need to talk and tell me what you took." I leaned back as he looked away. "And besides, what sort of Redcap Gnome doesn't talk much?"

"One," the words came slow and sluggish, "that has been in pain for too long."

I nodded. "That's a start. For how long? And again, what have you been taking for the pain?"

He sat in thought, looking out the window, perhaps listening to the all too common sound of sirens racing down the streets. "Two moons. Daily poppy and manticore salad." That explains the venom in his system, and two moons, he has been enduring this for almost two months.

"Look, Romeo, poppy contains opium, a very powerful painkiller, and manticore meat is poisoned with the same venom used in its' tail." I leaned forward again, typing into the computer to put this information in his charts. "It's probably making the Gem-Bumps worse as your body not only has to fight the disease but also the venom you're willingly ingesting. Without your salad, or with just the poppy, you could have been healed in a month."

"It's traditional medicine." Came the blunt response.

"But it's not true medication." I countered. "I want you to stay a few nights in the hospital, to detox, before we release you with a prescription for Ybuprogem cream. Directions will be on the bottle, but you rub it over your entire body, even where you don't have gems sprouting. Any questions?"

He sat in silence for a minute. "What will happen to the stones?"

I pulled up the information sheet on Gem-Bumps in the folder and scanned it. It had been over a year since I last saw a case of this and I could use the memory refresher. "They'll fall out. You can possibly sell the gems to help cover insurance or other bills you may accrue."

The glare he cast in my direction could be felt without needing to turn my head. I just shrugged. "Was just a suggestion, Mister Scareletcap." I closed the folder, tapping it on the desk a few times to set the papers within. Again, that act was mostly for show, since I hadn't dug in them too much. "However, the stay in the hospital is not a suggestion. I will alert the nurses and have the information go up the line as necessary. Good day."

He continued to scowl at me as I stood. "Doctor." He said, his thick voice accented. "I don't want to stay in a hospital."

"I'm not giving you a choice. I need to know that you're not going to continue eating your salads." I stopped at the door, turning to face him as he sat on the examination table.

"You don't want a Redcap angry at ya..."

"Threats now?" I shook my head. "Maybe you'll feel better after treatment." It was hard not to laugh.

He snorted, and was apparently starting to come down off the effects of everything he had been eating. "Do ya know what a Redcap does to those that piss him off?"

I set the folder down, and approached him quietly. "You really think your threats scare me, Gnome?" I hissed. "I have gotten more threats than you could dare to imagine, try me. My oaths do not mean I cannot defend myself."

Though he did not seem phased at my reaction, he did look away, out the window once more. I nodded and straightened. "That's what I thought." I muttered and turned, gathering the folder once again and walking out the door. This time I made sure the door was locked behind me, keeping the Redcap from escaping.

"Hope, get security please." I said, opening the folder and writing down the threats he made.

"Something wrong, Doctor Kadhäb?" She asked, picking up the phone and dialing.

I handed her the file. "Angry Redcap in room seven with a severe case of the Gem-Bumps alongside potential addiction to opium and manticore venom. Needs to be transported for a hospital stay to detox before he can begin the necessary treatment for his ailment."

She nodded and began repeating the information to security. The exchange took less then a minute before she hung back up. "They're on the way."

"Thank you, Nurse." I added with a smile. "Looking like I'm done for the day."

"Yea, you requested an early off again." She glanced at the screen. "Though I was hoping to get your assistance with some of the files before we open in the morning?" Her dark eyes swept up to mine. "There's a few discrepancies that I've caught that I'd like to clear up before quarterly reports are due."

You could just say that you want me early for a party. I thought, trying to keep a sly smile off my face. "Sure." I said, allowing the smile to come albeit more warm than sly. "I'll come an hour early, sound good?"

The young Elf beamed up at me. "That sounds ideal! Hopefully this won't take that long, maybe we can even go for coffee together before work?"

Now the smile on my face turned sly. "That... might be nice." I cleared my throat and started to unbutton my coat. "Though isn't there a policy about dating co-workers?" Not that Father would allow me to date. After all, he didn't want grandchildren from anyone other than his direct heirs.

She shrugged. "I never said *date.* I said go out for coffee, as friends and co-workers." She waved her hand in that feminine fashion. "Maybe even gossip a little. Whatever conversation that comes up."

"Let's see how fast we can clear those discrepancies first, shall we?" I suggested.

Hope laughed, the sound like music. Not a single person in the room, no matter their race, could withstand a smile coming to their face. "That sounds like a plan."

"I'll see you tomorrow, then." I shrugged the coat off my shoulders, turning to go to my office to gather my briefcase.

"Have a good rest of your day!" Hope called after me.

I simply waved as I entered my office. Down the hall, past the nurses desk, I heard the commotion of the Redcap Gnome being taken to the hospital against his will.

I wished I hadn't had to do so, bu failure to act would have cost me my license, especially if he wound up dead from an overdose or from mixture of medicines after seeing me. Alas, what was done, was done, and it would not do to dwell on the past.

Once I gathered my items into my briefcase, papers to go over, laptop to transfer information if I needed to work from home, and a few other odds and ends carefully positioned around a small pistol, I exited my office and made my way outside.

Even though the halls were busy no one actually stopped to say goodbye or anything akin. A few small waves, smiles, and nods were all anyone could spare. I was off for the day and headed home, everyone else was still working.

My ride home was as uneventful, though since I left earlier than normal I did have more crowds to circumvent. As always Sir Snowball was happy to see me, at least for a moment before turning back to his nap spot.

Tonight was my movie night, so I was glad to be home early. I tossed a bag of popcorn into the microwave and decided to do a quick run through of my emails before I sat down to watch whatever I felt like watching.

A couple emails from my fathers bodyguard, each saying simply:

Stan,

I've been trying to reach you. Please get back to me, it's important. Or if you don't, at least don't go to your Fathers' Birthday Party. I can't explain why, and I'm not sure you'd want to go anyway, just stay home. I'm sorry I can't say more in this email, but please, call me on your private line. You know which one I mean.

Yours in Service, as much yours as your Fathers,

Sir Ûlfin Strongarm

Head of Security, Bubbles Tower

Not the first time he sent me emails like this. And I was already planning on skipping the party. No need to contact him, the point was already made.

Besides, what else would he say? I thought sourly as I stood up, hearing the microwave ding in the kitchen. I started chuckling as my thoughts continued aloud.

"Oh, Lord Bubbles," I mocked the Orcs harsh Parydan accent, leaning heavy on every vowel. "it is needed that you go hide in the safe room this instant!" I flung the door to the microwave open a little too hard with a flourish. The door slammed back shut on me.

Sir Ûlfin Strongarm was the head of the Faryshan National Guard. He started under my grandfather, and was made the Chief Warrant Officer of the Pagoda Detail when my father took the throne. Recently he was made Head of the Guard, a title he wore with pride but rarely used. He was a friend growing up, but he was recognizable, and if I was seen around him someone would figure out who I really am.

I could not afford that.

So I cut him out of my life alongside everyone else. A necessity. One that I will continue to do as long as I can.

A pang of hurt went through me thinking of the Orc soldier. I quickly made sure the door wasn't broken before turning to grab a bowl from the cupboard for my popcorn.

Sir Snowball came running once he heard the food hit the bowl. Even though he had his own, I let him nibble on some popcorn alongside me. It was nice to have some company.

I brought the popcorn back in the office with me to finish filling out paperwork and scanning it in to email back to the office.

Sitting down he came and plopped his fluffy behind on my lap, a warm and vibrating presence. The work was done in short order before I picked him up in one arm, the popcorn in the other, and went into my living room. Sitting on the recliner I turned on the television as I patted his ears.

The news popped on, something about a threat made to the Bubbles family. I rolled my eyes. There was *always* a threat to the family. Every other threat made it to the news.

I promptly changed the channel. The movie was starting, something about some outer space war with red and green lazer and heat based weaponry.

I shifted slightly to make myself more comfortable. Sir Snowball yawned, patted at the little piece of popcorn I gave him, then curled around it with his eyes closing. Together we sat and, well, I watched the movie eating popcorn well into the night.

THREE

I took a breath before I opened the door to the darkened lobby. I was an hour early, as promised, and as far as I was aware, no one knew that I expected them to jump out at me as soon as this door opened.

To be fair, none of them knew I didn't like surprises, but that's fine. This little surprise party will make them feel happy, and to be honest, it warmed my heart as well, just knowing some people care about me.

I put on my best tired "I don't want to be here this early" face and opened the door.

"Surprise!" Came over a dozen voices all at once.

I smiled and chuckled. "A party!?" I exclaimed, honest humility coming into my features. "You didn't have to."

Hope came forward. "We wanted to. You've been here for a whhooole decade now! Plus none of us are actually sure when your birthday is, so we kinda jumped on this plan with gusto."

That made me chuckle. "You could have just looked at my records."

A rosy pink spread over her pale cheeks. "That would just be rude!"

"I told ya to do it!" A gruff voice came from behind her. Doctor Kronda Goldenbeard, an olive skinned Dwarf with bright golden-blonde hair braided into a beaded beard hanging down to his knees. "He probably wouldn't 'ave known if ya didn't say nothin."

I nodded down to him. "He's right. If you hadn't said anything I'd have assumed it just popped up on a calendar somewhere." My smile widened. "However, I am glad you put this together for me. I can't begin to explain how much this means."

Hope smiled and jumped into a hug. I faltered slightly but caught her, elves are always stronger than they seem. The hug felt nice, so I hugged her back for a moment.

Maybe I should ignore Fathers' orders and start seeing someone. Hope sure seems interested. I thought. It was a very warm thought as well. I sobered slightly. *But I don't want her to disappear.*

She broke contact and looked around. "Well, let's eat some cake!" She bounced off to the reception desk and pulled out plates to sit next to the cake on the desktop.

The cake was a simple rectangle cake with an image of a file folder with a stethoscope molded from fondant or some other molding material resting on top. A chocolate name badge that read "Doctor Stan Kadhäb, 10 years and going strong!" in painted lettering leaned against the metallic looking eartube.

Hope made sure I got the nameplate on my slice. The cake was chocolate. I'm not sure what my favorite cake flavor would be, I don't eat sweets that often, but I am sure that chocolate would be pretty high on the list. I accepted the slice and made a small show of trying to put the badge on my chest before awkwardly eating a slice without setting the plate down. The brown stain of chocolate on my shirt was worth the smiles.

Within the hour the cake was gone, beverages empty, and clean up was well underway. We couldn't leave a mess for our patients and their families, it would be highly unprofessional. Though everyone agreed to leave up a sign that simply read "Happy Ten Years Doctor Stan!"

The day went on as normal, though with the occasional well wishing from some parents. Little boy with a broken arm, distraught mother with stitches and a concussion from catching a jumping toddler, a couple dog attacks, and even a gunshot wound.

The last few were reported up the ladder as necessary. Guns especially as those are illegal in Farysha. I should say illegal for anyone not in security nor the Bubbles family. I kept mine in my briefcase. Of course that never stops the criminals from finding some and using them.

But yet the sirens went on. They will never stop. I found myself between patients wondering what it would be like to travel to another country. Bisney maybe with their long, sloping beaches coming down from the tall, black mountains. Or even Secqua with their colorful thick forests and brave griffon-riders.

I found myself staring into the distance, just tapping at my desk as the nurse cleaning up and sanitizing for the last patient was rambling on about something women talk about. I really was not paying much attention.

"Doctor, are you even listening?" Nurse Sera asked. She was human, with blonde hair and brilliant green eyes watching me, eyebrows creased in frustration.

I blinked a few times and focused from my thoughts of travel. "Sorry, zoned out."

"I was talking about the sirens, there's more than normal." She clarified.

I shrugged and looked at the file before me, as if I hadn't seen the papers before. "There's always sirens, some days there's more, other days there's almost none." I looked up from the words describing all the reasons why this particular patient was overweight. *To be honest she's probably overweight because of her diet more than any of these medical reasons....* I thought, looking at the hand written page of everything she wanted me to take into account at her visit. One of which was a completely sterile room which is what Sera was working on now. Not that our rooms weren't already as sterile as can be.

Sera looked back to her work, wiping off the examination table before speaking. "I guess you're right. It's always just worrisome when I hear any sirens."

"That's right, you're our new emergency nurse?" I noted, winking at her. "You sure you can handle it?"

The look she gave me was one that was fake shock and offense. She had only been here for a week. "You sure you can handle being a doctor?" I chuckled at the retort. "Ten years, must be doing something right." "Ha!" She snorted, seemingly accidental. "Give me a hand with this? The Orc will probably be rather irritated if we're late with her appointment."

I stood and started wiping down more surfaces. "She probably won't even notice. Orcs either notice everything, or are so dense that you can punch them and they won't feel it." I shrugged and pointed back towards her note. "With everything she claims she has wrong with her, probably the latter."

"Oh stop stereotyping, it doesn't become you. Or anyone, for that matter."

"Well, in my experience it's one of the truths about them." I said, mater of factly. "Besides, there's almost always some truth to stereotypes, else there wouldn't be one. Besides, why is she even in the emergency room and not at her PCP?"

"I gueessss you do have a point, and she was claiming chest pains though we could find nothing other than a slightly elevated heart rate due to her weight." She admitted. She pulled the paper out and straightened. "Well, this looks good enough."

"Either way she'll complain, willing to place a bet on that one."

She looked at me with an exaggerated fake gasp. "Doctor! Gambling is illegal!"

I chuckled. "And so is owning certain breeds of dogs, most drugs that we have access to and have to write prescriptions for when people who just want to abuse them are out, illegal if we don't." My smile faded to something more somber. "And so are many, many other things."

We stood in silence a moment, the humor taken out of the air. To be fair none of us remembered a time when there wasn't so many laws and restrictions. Such a time was past my grandfathers era, but everyone played along for various reasons. Mostly because they all valued life in it's basic form. I know I did.

Well, save for assassins and others who wanted to see change. They always met an early end though.

She looked down, almost ashamed. "Maybe one day I'll get out."

I couldn't look at her. "No one ever does that the Lord doesn't wish..."

Again, silence hung in the air, thick as fog off the sea. Sera fussed with the paper in her hand a moment before handing it back over to me. "I think I will go lead her in now."

I slowly nodded, "Yes, please." and took my seat. "Thank you, Nurse." I added, softly.

Kahrín Hamfist-Goldtusk squeezed into the room, sat on the examination table, and broke it.

The steel legs bent, drawers popped and cracked, and the padded top split under her weight. I wrote that down on her papers while she caught her breath. The State Insurance would send us a new table, they might even charge her for it. Either way this room will be out of service for at least a month or two while we waited for the system to catch up. *Maybe I could pull some strings, get it in faster...*I thought, watching her from the corner of my eye.

She was a Forest Orc, tall, green, with beady eyes and black hair in slicked braids. Two, small, tusks jutted out from her lower jaw, instead of the typical white they were yellowed with stains and one had a sick gray spot of a cavity forming. She would have a sort of wild beauty if she wasn't so grossly overweight.

"Miss Hamfist-Goldtusk," I started once she caught her breath. "what brings me the pleasure to see you today?"

"I am having issues getting rid of my baby-weight." She said. Her accent was subtle, she said issues as "is-sues" which noted her family had moved in from one of the more northern countries. I noted she said nothing of her chest pains.

"And how many children do you have?" I asked, pen in hand ready to take notes.

"Ten." She looked proud. "Youngest is two years now."

My eyebrows furrowed. "Any twins or triplets? You seem fairly young to have so many children at only thirty years of age." I glanced up from her papers before me.

"Nope!" The pride never left her face.

"And what have you been doing to try to control your weight?"

She thought a long moment. Far too long for someone actively trying to achieve their goal. "I've been dropping how much I eat." She said at last.

"Can you tell me how much you eat in a day?"

"A dozen eggs, a pound of bacon, two steaks, a scoop of mashed potatoes..." She trailed off.

Something was off, and the soft confusion more than likely shown on my face. "All day?"

"Oh no!" She chirped. "That's just breakfast!"

I groaned inwardly, checking that I didn't make an audible sound. "Please, continue then."

She did. Describing how for every meal she would eat a days worth of food, and how she wakes up in the middle of the night to eat more. How her kids and husbands don't look like her, that they're all bone thin but yet she can't get rid of the baby weight, so she must have some medical reason for it. "I just want to know what is going on so I can drop my weight again. I miss looking pretty." She at least looked honest.

I wrote down every bit of this. Almost every single person in Farysha had a card specifically for purchasing food. A certain amount, based off the size of your family and your job, was put on. All funded by the eighty percent tax most of the populous paid on everything. She would more than likely be seeing a decrease which will make this process easier in the long run.

"How would you like me to proceed?" I asked. "I like to avoid prescribing medication, though I do think you would see improvement with a change of diet and an increase of your daily activity."

"Nah," she snorted, "there has to be something else." She crossed her arms. "Can you do some blood tests?"

I slowly nodded. "I can..."

"Then I would like that please." She tried to wiggle, signaling that she was settling in to be more comfortable during a long wait.

I quietly sighed and hit the speak button connected to the nurses desk on the phone in the office.

"Yes, Doctor?" Came Seras' voice.

"Need a series of blood tests done please. Checking for thyroid and metabolism issues primarily alongside anything else that can cause gross weight gain."

"On it." She did not sound enthusiastic. I didn't blame her.

"Thank you." Kahrín smiled at me, smugly.

Nurse Sera came in and prepared to take the samples as I put the papers back together in the folder. "I will be leaving the room with the nurse to ensure that everything gets tested nice and fast for you." I smiled, trying to make it warm and friendly.

The Orc nodded. "I will wait here then?"

I nodded. "Please do. We will be back shortly."

After a few minutes and failed attempts to find a vein, Sera managed to gather the samples and we left, heading down the hall to the lab.

"Why did you say, we?" Sera asked.

"I am not going to tell her all the tests passed as fine and the only thing she needs to do is to put the fork down on my own." I admitted, looking over at her. "Have you not seen an enraged Orc? If she doesn't take the news lightly, well, let's just say I enjoy this little thing called life."

She chuckled as I opened the door for her. "That is true. I would hate to come in and see you squished against the wall."

A small laugh escaped me at the thought. "I guess I would hate that as well." I shook my head and set the folders down next to a lab tech. "It would hurt quite a bit."

Sera set the syringes on their tray next to the folder, nodded, and returned to the desk up front.

The lab tech, a small Gnome with a white cap tightly holding his hair in place and a golden thread holding his beard tight, glanced at the papers. "Let me guess," his voice abnormally deep, "has to have a medical reason as to why she's fat and came up with a fake reason to be here?"

"Spot on there." I admitted. "Test what you can, hopefully the test results will do what my words failed to manage."

"What," he spun in his chair and looked at me with an eyebrow raised, "that she needs to stop eating?"

"Exactly." I opened the folder and went over the papers again, force of habit now. "Just be fast and professional with this."

"Fine." The Gnome turned back to his work, fingers flying over the keyboard, finishing whatever he was typing before taking the syringes and hopping down, almost scuttling over to the machines on the other side of the room. "I'll send word to the nurses when it's done." He called over his shoulder.

"Thank you." I called back as I turned to leave.

Gnomes were amazing at the technical work, which is why the lab was almost completely Gnomes and one or two Fairies. Children thought they were adorable with their large hats and noses and beards trailing along the floor. While we did ask them to tie them so the long hair doesn't interfere with their work, one should never ask a Gnome to cut their beard. Doing so was a death sentence, though it's never exactly clear how.

I left the bustling room of little folk and returned to the nurses desk where Hope and Sera sat among others, ticking away at keyboards or sorting through files.

We took to chatting, asking each other what their favorite movies are and what they like about them, asking about small pets and other animals, where we want to go on vacation, and other small talk topics.

"So, Doctor," Hope changed the topic again. "you have any family? You don't talk about them and don't have any pictures in your office."

I stepped aside as another doctor came up and passed a folder to Hope, receiving another from a different nurse on the other side of the desk.

"I do," I started, "however they've sorta driven me out. It's a long story that I generally don't like talking about."

"Is that why you don't date anyone?" Sera chimed in.

I looked at her, eyebrow raised. "Hey, just because I'm not seeing anyone I work with does not mean I'm not seeing someone."

"So, who is she?" Sera stopped what she was doing and watched me, arms crossed over her chest.

"None of your concern."

She raised her eyebrows. "Oh really?"

"Yes, really." I knew that she was catching my bluff. I had a girlfriend at the University, but haven't really dated since we graduated and went our separate ways. She went to live in Peraspia far to the east. Or so I was told. I've been unable to find her since, and I did try a few times to reach out.

But the nurses didn't need to know any of that.

I shrugged before they could say anything else and went to my office. I had paperwork to finish off while we waited.

Of course as soon as I sat down and pulled out the first piece to sign off on, curse my procrastination, Seras' voice chirped on my phone set.

"Doctor, Miss Hamfist-Goldtusks' test results are in."

"Thank you, Nurse." I said, pressing the flashing button. "Have the papers ready, I'll be out in a moment."

I signed my name at the bottom of the paper, approval for a prescription, set it aside and left my office. Sera handed me the test results and I scanned them at the desk.

Everything tested normal. Her lifestyle was the only thing that was keeping her from loosing weight.

"Let's go tell her the bad news." I said to Sera.

"That everything tested normal and that you were right?" She asked with a flair. "Shall we go and hopefully not get killed by an Orc?"

"Let's." I gestured with my hand and we left down the hall to her room.

"Took long enough." Came the answer when I knocked on the door. Sera and I exchanged a nervous glance before entering.

"Well," I started, "we can't expect the lab to set aside what they were working on to focus on one patient, ma'am." I handed her the papers. "Test results show everything is normal. No health issues other than BMI."

"What does that mean?" She asked.

I sat down in my chair. "It means, that instead of prescribing you medication, I will be prescribing you a diet. I will be writing down various menus for you to follow through the day. Three meals of smaller size than what you're eating now."

She huffed in disagreement, but otherwise stayed quiet.

"Also I will be prescribing you a work out regimen, this includes a visit to a local physical therapy location. You are to follow these and you will see results." I leaned back in my chair, glad she hadn't moved much. "You will feel terrible for about a week, then you will start feeling better and will notice you have more energy. I will have the nurses," I nodded towards Sera, "have you schedule a check-up in a months time to ensure you're keeping up the regimen."

"What of my kids?" She asked.

"The PT location has a child-care program. We can schedule your visits to be while your elder children are at school so you can take the younger ones with you."

She nodded her agreement.

"Good." I stood up. "I will go and get the diet regimen for you prepared and will have that sent out shortly. You're free to go, just check in at the front desk for your next appointment."

"What if I don't follow them?"

I stopped from going out the door. "Then within the matter of a year or two you will more than likely be found deceased from cardiac arrest."

Confusion shown on her face. "I don't understand...."

"Ma'am," I sighed, "the short version is that you are so overweight that your heart is having problems functioning, so are your lungs and other internal organs. If they have not yet started they will soon start failing and the most logical conclusion is that, as a result you will probably have a heart attack and leave this world before you hit the floor."

She looked shocked that I would tell her that, so I continued.

"Listen, it's not a beauty thing like so many think, it's a health issue. Being overweight is not something to be proud of, it's dangerous. I have had so many women in particular come in, and not listen, and show up in the morgue. I'm not telling you this for anything other than if you don't change your ways you *will* die, and no one wants that, especially you or your children."

She glanced down, shamed. "I guess your right. Thank you for being honest. So many just tell us Orcs what we want to hear."

"Thank you for not getting angry." I nodded at her. "I need to go finish your paperwork, have a nice day."

I left the room and returned to my office, finishing up the paperwork for the day, pulling out a book of recipes and daily menus we keep on hand for this very reason, and left everything with the nurses desk on my way home.

The bike ride home was as normal. Riding on the road to avoid everyone walking, it's not like there's many cars out anyway, and those that were on the road had the owners name and an identification number on plates. Sirens rang out somewhere in the distance, smoke was somewhere as well.

At the apartment complex I chose to sit in the wooded area for a little bit, enjoying the birdsong in the relative silence. One can never truly escape the sounds of the city, even here in this small sanctuary. A couple people jogged by, nodding quickly as they passed me on the bench. A few couples meandered around, enjoying the break in city life this man-made forest offered. Each of them spoke in hushed, whispered tones to each other. I could have eavesdropped if I cared, but I chose to let their discussions remain private.

I wished I could travel more, see places like this in their natural form, hear true silence.

And while I would be allowed to travel, I didn't want to travel alone. No one would allow me to leave the country with another. I wouldn't allow myself to leave the country with another, they'd learn my true name at the border. They wouldn't want to be with me anymore.

With a suddenly heavy heart I stood, took my bike, and returned up to my apartment. Sir Snowball greeted me before returning to his perch.

I rummaged in my scarce fridge for a few minutes before deciding to order something. I didn't feel like cooking, nor did I have anything that I could cook.

Deciding to spoil myself, and because it lasts a while in the fridge, I ordered pizza and lemonade to be delivered. I didn't skimp either, I ordered a place that takes an hour to deliver because everything is made fresh down to the crust and hand squeezed lemons.

Knowing I had some time before I had to run down and meet the delivery person I decided to take a quick shower.

The water felt good running over my body, though it could not settle my mind. I felt sad, lonely. I wished I had someone. I was nearing forty years of age, and still I had no one to share my life with.

Remember, you have no one because your father would kill them. I thought. And it was true. I wasn't one of the heirs, anyone I had a true romantic relationship with would just disappear, probably into the slave trade if not the bottom of the sea.

I shook my head clear and stepped out of the shower, grabbing my plush towel and running it over my face and hair. I looked up and saw the hawkish features I inherited from my mother, suddenly glad I didn't look like Father.

Mother would never have followed through with these draconian edicts if she were in charge. My heart panged again as my thought process continued: if she were still alive. She was murdered when I was seven.

I held onto an image of her in my head as I tugged on my clothes. Slacks and a simple shirt, nothing fancy, I have to wear fancy every day at work and it gets tiresome after a time. After ten years.

I sat in my recliner, Sir Snowball jumping on my lap, and grabbed the remote. After a moment of staring at the black television screen I set it back down and grabbed my phone.

A message from the Bisney Pizza Shoppe said that delivery will be in about fifteen minutes time popped up. But no missed calls from Harry. I frowned, he had said he'd call back today. Normally he keeps his promises, it was one of the few good qualities he had. *He probably has to do something with his family,* I thought, *he'll call when he gets a chance.*

I gently pushed the fluffy white cat from my lap, much to his mewling displeasure, and stood. I slipped on some comfy shoes and grabbed my keys out of habit, hesitating a moment before placing them back down, heading to the elevator.

I only had to wait a minute or two before a delivery boy with bright red hair sticking out from under a cap rode up on a bike, the pizza and a jug tied to a flat rack on the back. He pulled up a yellow sticky note as I opened the door.

"Uuhh, Doctor Stan?" He asked, squinting at the handwriting on the note.

"Yup." I smiled and handed him some cash. "Keep the change."

"Thanks sir!" He smiled, pocketing the cash and handing me the pizza and jug. "You gonna be able to get that to your place alright?"

"I will, thank you." I smiled back.

He flicked the brim of his hat, a sign of respectful acknowledgment.

"Have a great day then, sir!"

I tilted my head at him and looked back, smile still on my face. "You too kid, keep up the good work." And turned to let the door close behind me.

"He seemed abnormally happy." I noted aloud, glancing around at the hallway.

The few people in the area were all smiling. It was an odd, but warming, site. Days like this didn't happen often, where people were just happy. It was a good day for it, warm and sunny weather. I presumed many were going to take the long ride down to the beaches on the public transport. I made my way up to my floor and awkwardly into my apartment. I set the pizza down in the little eating nook and put the jug next to the box. Sir Snowball came over, sniffing at the pizza.

"No buddy." I said as I picked him up and set him back on the floor. "You need to wait."

He meowed in disagreement, turning tail and walking back to his window-side tree bed. I grabbed a plate and put on a few slices for myself. A second, smaller plate I put a few toppings on for my spoiled cat. I set that plate on the floor by his food dish.

As soon as he heard it hit the floor he apparently teleported from the window to the dish, bumping the tall structure into the window with a loud thump on his way down.

"You should have been more careful there!" I scolded. He ignored me.

Shaking my head, I grabbed a cup, pushed it against the ice maker in the fridge door, and let it fill with ice before I filled it with the liquid gold that is lemonade.

With a warming mood I took my plate and cup and prepared to settle into my recliner once again, this time without my little white lap warmer jumping up. Holding a really hot piece of pizza in my mouth, seriously, who lets the stuff cool off all the way before eating, I set my plate down and grabbed the remote and flicked on the television as I turned to take my seat.

FOUR

The pizza and the remote hit the floor at around the same time, though I hardly took notice.

What was normally a channel with various movies now had Breaking News coverage. Smoke trailed up from the Red Pagoda, our capitol building and where I once called home. I counted at least three large plumes from various windows, and it appeared that every fire department in the city was on scene.

I shook my head clear and focused in on what the reporter was saying. "There is still no sign of the youngest child of the now former Lord Bubbles, though rumor has it that he had moved out of the Red Pagoda to study in the Archipelago University. We are awaiting word from him and from officials from the Pagoda itself."

Why would they be looking for me? I asked myself, too in shock to speak aloud.

I jumped when a loud knock came at my door.

"Stan?" A familiar voice called from the other side. "Are you home?"

"Ûlfin, you're.... How...?" I stuttered.

He cleared his throat on the other side of the door as I walked over. "I stopped by your office first, they said you came home. I rushed over here as fast as I could."

I opened the door to reveal a tall and well built Orc. Ûlfin Strongarm bent over and walked into the apartment. He took one sweeping gaze around as he closed the door. It paused as he took in the scene on the television and around the recliner, including my cat now trying to scamper off with the dropped pizza, leaving a red mark across the floor. He looked down, sadness creeping into his features, highlighting the wrinkles moreso than on any normal day. "You saw..." He muttered.

"What's going on, Ûlfin?" I asked. "Is this some sort of sick joke Harry played?"

"Assassins." He looked up, nodding to the side. "Though Harry did start most of the fires."

I chuckled softly. "Let me guess, he wanted to prove his strength and went after them, endangering everyone inside?"

Ûlfin nodded. "Exactly." He sighed, the sadness coming back to his features. "But the assassins succeeded, nonetheless. Everyone was together preparing for tomorrow, it was an easy target. Especially with Harry getting in our way throwing fire around like candy."

I turned away, looking again at my apartment, my home. Everything seemed so small, so fleeting. I looked back over my shoulder at the Orc. "The children?"

He didn't answer. Silence hung between us.

"The assassins?" I asked, whispering into the quiet air.

"Captured, awaiting your command."

My command. On my word I could send their souls into oblivion. I could have them tortured to the brink of death. I could release them. I felt sick to my stomach.

"Just...." I trailed off, not sure what to do, how to react. I wasn't trained for this, Harry was, Jasmine was, their kids.....

Their kids were too. "just leave them in the dungeon for now. Figure out who sent them, and why." I finished.

Oddly, I was glad that my nieces and nephews were not going to be raised to be evil like the rest of my family. They weren't going to get the chance to take over the bureaucracy, to squeeze everything they could out of the people of Farysha. Their souls could be born again, start over with a good family. They could be good in another life.

But it wasn't this life. It wouldn't be with me as their uncle coming when they scraped their knees, broke an arm. No more would I see their smiling faces, unaware of the horrors that awaited them. The actions they would one day force upon innocence.

I stumbled towards my chair and sunk in. Ûlfin watched me, his face stone still though I thought I saw a hint of concern in his dark blue eyes.

Leaning forward I rested my face in my hands, trying to keep a hold on my heart rate, on my thoughts, on my tears.

I failed.

Ûlfin stood there, watching me as tears silently fell through my fingers, realization settling into me.

My father was never the nicest person, but he was still my father and was the only parent I had left. He was going to be in his nineties tomorrow.

I'm not sure how long I sat there, how long Ûlfin stood there. At some point he said something into a military style microphone, but I wasn't paying attention to what.

When I finally managed to get a calming breath, clear my head, and look up the sun was low in the sky. Darkness and curfew was settling over the city, and Sir Snowball had eaten the rest of my pizza and was eyeing up my now warm glass of lemonade. It looked like Ûlfin had a slice or two as well, some red stood out against the paler green of his skin at the corners of his mouth.

He noted my stirring and his eyes and attention snapped to me with decades of professional practice. "Lord Bubbles?"

I shook my head, sickened again to hear the title directed at me. "No, Ûlfin, just Stan. Please. At least for now."

He nodded, expression somber. "As you wish."

I took another deep breath. "What about my job?"

He shrugged. "You are Lord now, you do not need to be a doctor."

"It's who I am." I shook my head, trying to avoid the urge to return to my silent tears, hiding them poorly behind my hands still wet. "If I can't go back we need to tell the office."

He thought for a moment, his dark brow furrowing more deeply than that of a humans. "I know you went by a false name to protect your reputation. We could release official papers or such along the lines to announce "his" death, freeing you of obligation." He suggested.

The thought of more death, albeit a fake one this time, still sickened me. I must have paled visibly for Ûlfin continued to speak.

"I could also go in, or have another messenger do so, and announce your true identity and speak the truth. Gathering any personal items for you in the process."

I thought of Hope, how heartbroken she would be in either case. There just was not a good way to proceed. Even if I had word sent that I was to work as the personal physician to the new Lord Bubbles, they would see my face before the end of the day and learn the truth.

The guards wouldn't let me go down in person either. They would call it a security risk and block me every step of the way. The Lord Bubbles never left the Pagoda.

That would have to change. Many things will.

"Have a messenger send word of the truth and collect my items. Make sure he expresses my deepest apologies in regards to the lie I had to tell. No one would accept me if I used my true surname, but they did my false. They trusted Doctor Kadhäb, I hope they will trust me as Lord Doctor Bubbles as well. There will be changes in how things are done, hopefully for the better. I am not my father, nor will I be." The words were more for myself to hear than for the message. I needed the re-enforcement and I knew no one else, save Sir Snowball, was going to say it.

Ûlfin nodded, "I will get the word out and send a messenger in the morning. Shall we have a grand elevation?"

"NO!" I shouted, startling my cat to took off towards the bedroom. I took another breath. "No." I said, calmer. "It's not something we should use taxpayer money on. We can be simple and quiet and get down to work faster."

He nodded again. "I will have someone collect your items tonight then. Would you like to redecorate the Penthouse?"

I thought for a moment. "Some of it." I straightened in my chair, stiffening my back as I was taught long ago and used when I needed an extra aura of authority in the office. "I want to wait a little before I fully decide, though I do want the main bedroom to resemble mine here, with everything from my own room here to be transferred."

He repeated my words into his microphone pinned near his shoulder. Affirmation came from the other end.

"We will also note your landlord of your departure and ensure that he is paid well for rent due and for his success in keeping you safe."

I snorted. "He was keeping me safe?"

Ûlfin shrugged. "He may not have known, though his security systems did ensure no one could break in even if they wanted to. We did also make sure that he was unaware of your true identity, as per your requests."

"Thank you, Ûlfin, I know my father would have had it the other way."

He shook his head. I raised my eyebrow in surprise, cocking my head to one side.

"It was his idea, Stan. He wanted you to be safe." He watched as I leaned back forward, resting my forearms against my knees. "He thought something like this tragedy would happen. Once your mother passed, he knew he had to convince you to leave. His way of doing so was.... Not ideal.... But he knew you could survive if the others could not."

I rolled my eyes. "Convince me to leave? Try shipped me out to school most of my life." I grumbled.

Ûlfin nodded, slowly. He understood. He was there. He saw everything. Every argument, every word said in anger. I didn't have to explain to him what happened. Why I thought the way I did. The man was close to retirement as is, the last thing he needs is for me to whine about my past.

Sir Snowball mewed at me from the hallway, poking his head out of a room. I watched him for a moment. He was getting upset that we weren't going to bed yet.

"His carrier is in the closet of the office, Ûlfin. Can you please grab it?" I asked.

The orc started moving, a slight acknowledgment nod in my direction as he did so. I got up as well, grabbing a can of tuna from a cabinet and draining the liquid as he came back out, carrier tiny in his hands. He set it down and I placed the can in the back.

Sir Snowball could not resist this rare treat. He bolted into the carrier, eating like he hadn't eaten at all today. Quietly I was able to shut the door and stand up with it, setting the carrier on a table.

"I would like my clothes brought over first." I told Ûlfin as I walked towards my bedroom, stopping only to grab my briefcase.

"It will all be transferred at more or less the same time." He said. "Do not fret over the move."

I didn't respond, I did not feel there was a need to. I took a backpack from my closet, and began filling it with my pajamas, my medical travel kit, and some changes of clothes. I knew the crews would have everything moved relatively fast, however I wanted to make sure that if there was a hiccup in the transfer I wouldn't have to wear the same thing for a few days.

I sat on my bed. In either case I wouldn't. I could go have anything I wanted brought to me at any point. I was the Lord Bubbles now. Lord of Farysha. Lord of Hykur. I was Stan Bubbles, Evil Overlord with a Medical Doctorate.

I didn't want to be. Again the tears came. This time I was alone on my bed. I let them. I have seen others grieve, I knew it was normal. If I didn't let it happen it would only stew and fester, becoming something dark and ugly.

There was enough dark and ugly in the world. I didn't want to add to it.

I didn't cry as long as I did earlier, and quickly composed myself and stood, shrugging into the backpack.

Ûlfin raised an eyebrow at me as I walked out. "I can carry that for you." He offered.

I shook my head no. "I can carry it." I took one last look around at my apartment. My eyes landed on what remained of the pizza and lemonade, stomach turning at the thought of grabbing a slice to eat on the way up, denying me more food.

I sighed sadly, turning to the door and leaving my apartment, and my former life, for one last time.

And, avoiding the car waiting for me, the new Lord Bubbles walked himself up the mountainside to the Red Pagoda, a massive Orc bodyguard behind him with a small cat carrier in his hands.

FIVE

I spent the night awake in my old room. The bed was too small, sheets too stiff, and mind too awake.

I didn't want to sleep in my fathers bed, especially on the night of his death. The thought was awkward and sickening.

So I slept in my old room, once shared with my older brother Aaron. His old childrens items still remained. While he had gotten a similar treatment from our father as I did, he wasn't chased out or sent away to other schools in the Archipelego, just boarding schools in Farysha.

I wasn't certain if I believed Ûlfins' words or not. That Father actually cared for me and wanted me to be the one to survive in case of an emergency. If he truly did would he not have had me stay in the Archipelago? Would he not have married me out to a foreign dignitary as he had my sister?

So many questions. Not many of which would ever be answered.

Again grief hit. I had been going between tears and doubt all night, so when they started again I was prepared and rolled to the side, allowing them to fall freely.

I cried in silence as I had all night since my arrival. No one knocked at my door. No one asked for my attention. My father was so draconian that they knew better. Or maybe they were not completely dead inside and knew that I needed this to heal.

Evil family or not, this still hurt.

It took an hour or so before I was able to compose myself and leave the room, freshly dressed with my hair combed out. I didn't need to comb it, but the process aided in the calming effort.

Slowly I made my way into the living area. The Penthouse of the Red Pagoda was immense. Ten bedrooms, two living rooms, two dining rooms, multiple offices, and a commercial kitchen just to start. Chefs were already working away, creating food for myself and all those whose jobs it was was to keep the Penthouse clean, safe, and to ensure my orders were followed to the letter.

Everyone moved out of my way as I walked into the dining room closest to the kitchen. I was still in a slight daze, I barely noticed. I sat down in my old spot at the long table, almost in the middle instead of in the fancy chair at the head. The chair that would be my proper spot to sit at now.

I heard whispers around me, but no one dared correct my choice of seating. I almost dared them to try. I knew what they were about.

Ding dong the Lord is dead. My thoughts chimed. Everyone was happy because of the tragedy. Part of me was as well, as much as I hated to admit it.

At the same time they were worried that I would follow in my fathers footsteps. Or that I would be even worse.

Few knew me, and those that did looked at me with hope. Everyone else looked at me with fear, or with deadpan silence.

I rested my elbows on the table and leaned my face into my hands. I wasn't sure if I had so much to live up to, or so much to avoid living up to.

Another deep breath kept my mind clear and my breathing calm. I had no more tears to cry, and too much work to do to continue this... this what? Process?

I sighed heavily. Sleep deprivation wasn't helping my thoughts. I could keep my mind clear all I wanted, but I needed to make sure my choices were right and not mistakes.

I looked up when I felt the aura of someone approaching. I glanced to the side without moving my head all the way, trying not to glare for being disturbed.

It was one of the servants who ensures everyone is fed. He bowed as he approached. "Lord Bubbles." He murmured.

I nodded. "Speak." My voice came out dry and cracked a little. I coughed slightly, trying to adjust my throat and fix it.

"What would you like to eat, M'Lord?" He asked, still bowed.

"Stand up." I whispered. "I don't need that hyper formal shit." I cussed, something I normally don't partake of but not really caring at the moment.

I waited until he straightened, looking awkward the whole time. Once he settled some I continued, "I will take whatever the chef has made already. I won't have him go out of his way to make anything special for me."

The waiter nodded and bowed again, backing up as he did so, bumping into someone else. The lady he hit fell over, dropping the tray of glass water goblets and falling upon it.

I sighed and shook my head as I jumped to my feet. "Stop that hyper formality. Look where you're going." I helped her up gently, checking her injuries. "Get someone to clean this up and to grab my cleaning and suture kit from my med bag in my backpack."

With the small lady in my arms I rushed her into the kitchens and to a currently empty sink. The chefs and their assistants gawked as they moved aside.

"What was in the goblets?" I asked her, starting the water to run hot.

"C-coffee, mostly." She stuttered, in shock and pain. "Some lemonades made with fruits and a tray of meats, cheeses, and crackers."

I nodded and glanced over as a servant appeared with my decent sized bag blazoned with a large, red cross on the top.

"Open it," I addressed the servant, "and hand me the needles and threads." I looked to the lady. "Some of the glass went pretty deep into your hands and arms, but thankfully nothing hit a major artery."

As the servant, a young man with pale blonde hair, pulled open the bag and made a mess of it I directed the lady to hold her arms over the sink, allowing me to turn them ever so slightly to assess where the larger shards were and what needed attention first.

"Ma'am," I said, "I'm going to need to pull out the glass right before I stitch each wound. Some of these will only need to be bandaged, but this will sting and I need you to be absolutely still." She wobbled slightly in my arms and I shouted over my shoulder to have a stool brought over for her and for someone to help hold her steady.

My words were obeyed with haste and no questions.

As soon as I was handed the needle and threads the stool was brought and another person entered the room, a large red cross blazing upon his shoulder. He stood in the doorway, glowering at me as I worked on the lady's arms.

One by one I pulled out the pieces of glass, cleaned the area, and stitched it shut. Once I got to the smaller ones I started using water proof bandages.

Within the hour the process was done and she sagged against the sink, barely conscious. I washed my hands, scrubbing up to my elbow as a force of habit before cleaning my tools and putting my bag back together when the other physician approached.

"One should not steal anothers' job." He grumbled. Those still in the kitchen stared in shock at such an open remark.

I straightened to my full height. I wasn't tall, but I could get an extra couple of inches if I wanted to by how I stood. I looked the other man in the eyes as I spoke. "Before I was Lord I was Doctor. I did my job." He looked down. "And besides, it is also my job to protect my subjects. She was hurt and needed attention. I did my job. You stood by and watched as someone made a mess of my bag, I'm certain is the exact copy of one you have. Instead of assisting, you stood by."

Guards appeared like silent wisps behind the doctor. I waved them down, but did not release my stare. "Now, you speak out against my actions."

I let those words hang in the silence, watching the man before me pale. I understood why, he was newer, and did not recognize my face.

He understood that any other Lord Bubbles would have had him executed on the spot for speaking out against me as he did.

But I would not be my father.

Once I felt my point had sunk in I lowered my voice to a more gentle tone. "Look, I'm not going to hurt you because of your actions." The relief on his face was visible. "But," I continued, "should something like this were to happen again, I expect you to step up and help, not stand by and do nothing. Together, one on each arm, we could have had her tended to faster."

His head still hung in shame, though now he was more relaxed knowing I spared his life.

"Go do your job, and let me do mine." I allowed a growl enter my voice in my dismissal of the man.

The guards watched him scamper off, glancing at me holding the medical bag. I waited a few moments before exiting the kitchen as well. Many servants and assistants were standing outside the door, watching. Word had apparently spread that I had helped the lady instead of yelling for her to be removed from my sight. That I had not executed a man who had dared speak out against me.

For once I saw something shining in each of the eyes watching me: hope. Hope that I was different. My heart panged thinking of the word, of the nurse, of the life I was forced to leave behind.

"Listen up," I announced, "things will be different. I know my family has always had strict rules, laws, and mandates. That changes." I looked around at all the faces staring at me. "Today we got lucky, that young lady could have met serious injury had she landed on the glass shards differently than she did. So no more always facing me, no more backing away. Speak your mind if you feel it necessary. These things will not be met with punishment." I started forward to the room where I had set my backpack and briefcase.

SIX

Breakfast was fresh, hot, and simple. I ate like I hadn't eaten in a week. I felt better, calmer, afterwards, and Ûlfin had come to eat besides me. For a while we had eaten in silence before he remarked on my actions earlier.

He was proud.

We savored the silence of the morning, despite people of many races bustling around, ensuring the Pagoda ran smoothly. Both of us knew that once we got up, there was work to be done.

Sure enough, as soon as I stood my plate vanished back to the kitchens and I swiftly made my way to my office.

The desk was empty.

I pulled an assistant running by aside.

"M'Lord." She bowed deeply. "What can I do for you?"

"Why is there no paperwork on my desk?"

She looked at me, confused. "There has never been paperwork on the Lords Desk. Brock, the Head of Administration, handles all the paperwork."

"Tell Brock I want to see the most important papers on my desk. I want to know where spending is going, and the list of laws and mandates that he thinks need to be dealt with." I looked around, noting the guards as well. "I also want a poll to be done within our military forces on how they think we can improve."

She bowed and took off down the hall the direction she came from. I propped the door open and sat behind the grand desk, noting the amount of lotion and tissue paper on it's top. I put the lotion in one of the empty garbage cans next to the desk. I felt sickened at the plural of garbage canS. No wonder this was always the do not disturb room.

Within minutes Brock appeared in the doorway, an armful of papers in folders and a scowl on his face. I looked down at the Dwarf with his bright red hair braided and held in place with intricate, golden beads. This was a man used to working and being listened to by sheer reward of honest respect.

"Lord Bubbles wants to do paperwork now?" He asked, his voice low and gruff.

I shrugged. "I'm used to paperwork and want to be an actual decent leader. I'll go insane with nothing to do but apparently jack off in my office."

He didn't react to the comment. "Well, if ya want to help, here." He stood on his toes and slid the stack of papers across the tall desk. "Just don't mess anything up."

I chuckled. "I'll do my best, Brock."

He smiled warmly. "Good. An' if ya need help ya send a runner."

We nodded at each other and he walked off, messing with his beard a moment before snagging someone rushing past and barking some orders in regards to some plumbing that needs to get done and hasn't been yet.

I leaned back in the chair and opened the first folder.

In Regards to the Murder of the Prince Eryk Lision of Bisney, Husband to now and former Princess Liliana Bubbles of Farysha. The title read. Below was a list of actions that needed to be completed to keep King Jean appeased.

First off I needed to write a letter, then I had to either execute the assassins or send them to him to execute himself. I had an idea, but I needed to make sure I had everything right.

I called Ûlfin into the room. The Orc bowed as he entered.

"Ûlfin, has there been any word on the identity and orders of the assassins?"

"Yes, Stan." He nodded as he spoke. "Martin Broadshoulder and Aeshley Hyklin. Sent from the High Chieftain of Paryda."

"Has either confessed to killing specifically Prince Eryk?"

"Aeshley confessed to the murder."

"Prepare to send her to King Jean please." I looked down and sorted the papers a little bit, pulling a blank piece of vellum from the folder. "I will be sending along a formal letter, I will be sending another to the High Chieftain as well."

Ûlfin bowed and left, ensuring my orders were to be followed.

I grabbed my pen and leaned over the Vellum,

To King Joan Lision, Monarch of Bisney,

This is a time of grief we both share. You, for your lost son, and myself for my lost family. As our families were united together with the wedding of Prince Eryk to my sister, Liliana, so we stand these days. As a token of good faith I send this letter with the assassin that took the life of your son to see punishment as your laws dictate.

I send my deepest condolences for your loss. I cannot begin to imagine the loss of ones' child. If desired I will return his body to you alongside that of my sister, his wife, for Binsian Customary Funerary Rites.

If there are any matters you wish to discuss further you have every permissions to call my direct lines. As my family has been in good relations with you in the past, so would I prefer to see these relations grow in a positive manner.

Let us Live in the Memory of Those We have Lost,

Lord Stan Bubbles, M.D.

I slid the vellum into an envelope and sealed it with the wax Seal of State, a sleeping dragon upon a chevron, and set it aside for Ûlfin to pick up before the prisoner transfer.

The next folder I almost threw across the room as soon as I saw the title:
Coronary Report: Casualties of Red Pagoda Terrorist Attack
The official causes of death of everyone who passed in the attack. My father, my brothers, sisters, nieces, and nephews.
I stared at the folder, unable to bring myself to open it.
Instead I turned around in the swivel chair and pushed it to the filing cabinet, folder in hand. I opened the cabinet to nothing but rows of pornographic magazines, something that is heavily outlawed in Farysha. Rolling my eyes I grabbed some tissues and started to pull the magazines out and put them in the trash.
Ûlfin came in and watched me for a time before he chose to make his presence known by clearing his throat.
"I am aware that you're in the door." I said, glancing over my shoulder momentarily. "Letter for King Jean is on the desk. The one to High Chieftain Ukzahg will be written later. Can you send someone to sanitize the filing cabinets in here? Unsanitary does not begin to describe these...." I trailed off.
The Orc let out a deep, rumbling chuckle. "One of the family *traditions* I am glad to see gone." He admitted. "Someone should be in shortly."
He bowed quickly and left, letter in hand. Almost seconds after he left a servant came in, a spare trash can and arms filled with cleaning supplies. I furrowed my brow. "No basket to carry your supplies?"
He shook his head no.
"Well," I went back to cleaning out the cabinet I was at, he went to another and pulled on rubber gloves to pull out the magazines. "I suppose that is something I will have to fix."
"Thank you, M'Lord." He muttered.
"Can't have those who do important work like keeping the Pagoda and Penthouse clean wandering around with no way to carry their supplies."
"Guess not, sir."

Together we cleared and sanitized the filing cabinets. He even found new labels to replace the current labels. Tags like "Bisnian Beauties" will not work for filing actual paperwork.

We leaned back, the full trash can between us. "Before I dismiss you I would like to request that, once I retire to sleep, that a cleaning crew come in and finish sanitizing the office. I would hate to find more.... Surprises.... Like this."

He laughed quickly, but stopped himself and bowed deeply. "Sorry M'Lord, I could not help myself."

"You're fine." I smiled. "I'm not as strict as my predecessors."

He opened his mouth to say something, thought a moment, and closed it, instead preferring to gather up the cleaning supplies.

"What is it?" I asked.

Red flushed over his ears. "Nothing, sir. It was something that would have been rude to say."

Something thrummed deep down in me, some hurt, some anger. I pushed it down, whatever it was it was inappropriate. "You are dismissed then, just do not forget that I want this room sanitized and all the porno crap out of here."

He bowed deeply, some cleaning supplies spilling from his arms, before gathering up what fell and promptly leaving.

I shook my head with a sad sigh and returned to the paperwork. Next up was approval for funeral proceedings and options as to what we could do.

Everything is so expensive... I thought, looking at descriptions of parades to grand palisade mausoleums.

Last on the list was a simple funeral pyre. I circled that option and signed my name, adding a note to reserve the Prince and Princess of Bisney until we receive word from the King.

Fire with death has always had a special place within our culture. Pyres are normally saved for great leaders or heros, an odd representation of the volcano in the center of our country, surrounded by our valleys and the Black Mountains. I felt my nieces and nephews deserved it more than other members of my family.

It also served as a reminder, for everyone, that no matter how mighty you are that you can still fall. In the end we are nothing but dust gathering on this planet.

I continued on the paperwork until the sun was high in the sky. Somehow I was able to return to my professional state of mind, keeping emotions in check the entire time. I had but a few folders left to sort though, most were ready to be sorted back out to wherever they needed to go, and many were placed into properly labeled filing cabinets.

I sat at my desk a moment longer, running my fingers over the woodgrain. I paused, knowing I should rise and eat some lunch, but not wanting to move. Slowly I pulled my phone from my pocket and checked it, wishing there was a message from Hope or Sera. Wishing they would say that they understood, and that they didn't hate me for lieing to them.

Wishing I didn't hurt them beyond repair.

Nothing had come in, from anyone. I pulled out the laptop and logged into my email.

Again, nothing.

I tried logging into my work email, hoping that something was there, that those I left behind didn't leave me behind. I couldn't log in. I had been removed from the system.

I didn't realize I had done any magic until the door slammed shut, my vision clouding.

I just lost my entire family, and no one can reach out. No one could check on me.

No one cared.

I shoved those thoughts deep down. They were probably in as much shock as I have been. A friend turned out to be someone else, new leadership, fear that he secretly is just as bad as his father before him.

There was a heavy knock at the door, someone trying to get it. I fused the auras of the door and frame tighter to the wall. I didn't want to talk to anyone. The laptop screen flickered, **Invalid Login** still blaringly large on the display.

I glared at the door, not wanting to move out of sheer spite and anger. "Stan!" Ûlfin called from the other side of the door. "Stan! What's wrong?!"

Was that worry in his voice? I shook my head. Something was wrong, this wasn't me. I never reacted in anger.

I took a calming breath, something that was quickly becoming a force of habit, and released my magical hold keeping the door shut.

The door flung open and the large Orc fell into the office, not expecting the sudden lack of resistance.

I stood and went to him, ensuring he wasn't hurt. He pushed himself up on his hands and knees. "Sorry, Ûlfin. I don't know what came over me."

"What happened?" He asked, a soft growl in his voice from his heavy breathing.

"I...." To be honest, I wasn't sure exactly what was going on. More than likely my hunger coupled with my grieving spurred me to overreact. I sighed, looking over to the desk with the laptop and phone sitting atop it. "I think I need to eat something and take a break from paperwork."

His blue eyes watched me, not believing the words I said for one moment.

I looked away from his gaze, ashamed. "It was an unnecessary outburst of anger. Food should help." Though I was not hungry anymore, I knew the need to eat and understood the term many had coined "hangry" for when you forget to eat and have bursts of anger like this as a result.

He stood, the look still smoldering in his blue eyes. Quietly I stood as well, leaving my phone and laptop where they were and closing the door to the office behind me as we left.

I didn't want to talk, I didn't know what to say. I scared the man, I probably scared all of security with my actions.

As we sat down in the middle of the table and servants began to bring food out I found myself once again wishing that nothing had changed. That Harry was still alive and assuming the throne. That Jasmine was still inheriting the business.

That their kids were here running around, filling the Penthouse with laughter.

That anyone truly cared.

SEVEN

As tedious as paperwork was, it was nice to get back into the monotonous job. I was able to, at least for a time, forget my worries, my sorrows, and work on fixing the errors my family made. Many budgets set for lavishes, but few set aside for necessities such as cleaning supplies. Signing off that the Board of Directors for Bubbles Toys was not going to change under my new leadership and that they retained their prior authorities over the business, freeing myself of needing to watch it like a hawk.

Brock, true to his word, came whenever I sent a runner asking for assistance. Mostly it was questions like "How did the budget for so many pornos get approved and where in the heck are they kept so we can destroy them?" and "What does this even mean; *Savings for a Sunny Day?*"

To each he would answer usually with "It was never my place to question what the Lord desired, sir." and followed up with both of us agreeing to stop spending money on such matters, or to transfer the funds to somewhere else that could use them.

And as we did so, bedrooms were rearranged to guest rooms, their former contents placed into storage in case they were needed for future children, the Master Rooms were set up as my bedroom in my apartment had been, and wood and other items needed were gathered for the pyres.

Word had been sent to the High Chieftain, asking why he chose to assassinate the entire family, potentially offering the life of his assassin in return to be left alone. We still awaited his response along with that of King Jean.

I was impressed on how fast everything was getting done. By day two of my new life, there was visible improvement on not just the decor of the Penthouse, but also the moods and faces of those who worked within. It was a small step, but an important one.

So it was that nearing the end of that second day Ûlfin entered with a folder from the Farysha Military Forces: the results of the poll I requested.

Small nods to each other and he returned to other business, leaving me alone with no one save the guards outside the door who had taken to following me around, ensuring no one would kill the first Lord Bubbles they actually liked to serve.

The results were compiled into graphs, showing first an approval rating nearing that of twenty percent followed by the top suggestions.

✗ Need to train with the weapons we use in battle.

✗ Ways to increase morale.

✗ Better wages.

The list continued though many were similar reiterations of the top three. At least the first one was easy enough to manage immediately as I gave the others more thought.

Reaching into a freshly organized drawer I pulled out a sheet of parchment, saving the vellum in the drawer underneath for larger matters of state. Setting it on the desktop I quickly went about using my best script, one of the few things Mother ensured I learned, wrote an edict that all arms forces are to immediately begin training with their weapons, even in times of peace, so that they are best set to defend the country against all threats.

This I signed, sealed, and set aside for Ûlfin himself to deliver. The Orc was quickly becoming my most trusted guard and assistant, and already word of such has been spreading through the ranks.

Looking up I spotted Brock outside my door, pointing and muttering something to two different runners trying to go in opposite directions. When they were sorted out and went where the small Dwarf seemed to approve of he turned to enter the office, scoffing at the guards small attempt to stop him. His visits have become frequent enough that they knew better than to fully stop him. The greaves of one of the men still had a sharp dent from Brocks' heavy boot.

He bowed stiffly once he crossed the threshold and promptly approached my desk.

"Sir, letter for you from Bisney." He slid it across the desk until it was halfway to me and he could not push it further.

I set down the sheets I was brainstorming upon and grabbed the letter with its' elegant wording.

Lord Bubbles, Leader of Farysha, Doctor of Men,

I have received your letter and gift of good faith. The assassin, for her name is not worth bearing in Our golden scripting, has been promptly dispatched by my hand.

There is much yet we have to discuss.

Please, prepare the pyres for Eryk and Liliana. I will be following t his letter promptly.

I eagerly await our meeting, though I do wish that it was under better circumstances.

En Ce Regardious Mijore,
King Jean Lision

I stood from the desk with haste and beckoned Brock to follow as I not quite stormed out of the office, letter in hand.

"M'Lord, what is it?" Brock asked, huffing as he tried keeping up to my longer strides.

"News," I answered, not looking from my path to the main living area, "much to do and not enough time to do it." I paused near the door. "Get everyone in here, and make sure that the final pyre I was unsure of preparing is prepared."

Realization sparkled in his eyes and he bustled down the halls, barking orders to gather in the main hall.

I entered the room and looked around. The entrance to the Penthouse, a door to the stairs and another to the still broken elevator, were on one end, various hallways branched from the walls and the larger of the dining areas stood at the other. I walked in that direction, hopping onto the table so all could see me. I could use magic to ensure all heard me.

Within minutes the hall was filled with beings of all races, waiting to hear what I had to say.

"Listen up," I started, using magic to enhance the aura of my voice so all could hear without me shouting, "I just received word from the King of Bisney. Part of what I have to say will be orders to be followed, you will hear why."

I held up the letter, golden words glinting in the light alongside the royal seal holding shimmering ribbons of silks.

"We are expecting at least one guest possibly tomorrow or the day after. The King of Bisney himself and more than likely guards and retinue. I have never had to go through these proceedings, so we all need to work together to keep myself from screwing up and insulting His Majesty by accident."

That comment was met with chuckles across the hall. I paused, letting the humor fade slightly.

"Now, I know that the spare rooms of the Penthouse are prepared for guests. I know that we also have a separate guest suite within the Red Pagoda a floor or two down that needs some work."

I looked to the team of men standing in a door to a hall, wearing the shirts of builders and fixers. "First I need men and women to ensure that the suites are prepared and ready for any of the Kings retinue that cannot fit within the Penthouse. I don't want any beds falling nor fires started because of anything faulty."

Next I found the kitchen staff. "Next I understand that we will have need for at least one great feast, assuming once the funeral pyres have faded. We will also be needing to feed the King and Retinue over the course of their entire visit, which the extent of has not been made clear."

I looked back over the entire room. "My apologies for how last minute this is, I summoned everyone once I finished reading the letter. It is my assumption that they are currently on the way." I paused, looking for a particular, tall Orc.

Ûlfin was standing near the back, having recently come back up the steps from the lower level. He nodded to signal I had his attention. I signaled that I wanted to talk to him once this is over, or rather to ensure an order was passed to High General Ahun.

"Ûlfin," I continued, once the quick signal passed from my hand, "please have the border patrol alerted to their arrival. I would see the King and Retinue properly and politely escorted to the Pagoda. Also have them send word ahead to the first person who would answer."

Once again my gaze swept the room, taking in every face looking up at me. "Whoever hears this news ensure that everyone else is aware. Together we can have the whole Pagoda ready within the day. I expect his arrival will be at some point tomorrow. Each of you has already proven yourselves to me in your abilities to work with haste and quality. If we need to then contract other businesses in Hykur to assist. I doubt we have time to receive aid from the other cities."

I paused, thinking of what else there was to say. Just one more thing. "Thank you, everyone. Together we can do this, and without your help I would be left squandering about what to do. You are dismissed, show me that I am right in your talents."

I jumped off the table, stumbling slightly at the landing and falling on my rear. Brock came to me first, looking me at eye level. "I will get books fer ya on yer desk." He said. "Read em, they describe the proper procedures for what we're about to do."

"Thank you, Brock." I stood as Ûlfin approached. "We have much to do and not enough time to do it in."

The Dwarf bowed and scurried off, barking orders to others as he went, conducting what could have been utter disaster like a master before an orchestra. I watched him in awe for a moment before turning to Ûlfin and speaking in a hushed tone.

"There is a letter for High General Ahun upon my desk. It contains orders to ensure that our troops are training with the gear they use in battle."

A deep eyebrow raised. "They only train with them when we are in war." He leaned closer. "Are we in war?"

I shook my head, taking a moment to glance around. "I hope not, but now would be a good time to attack us. Besides, I think I would sleep better at night knowing we were prepared for an attack rather than sitting ducks with none but the Guards armed. It might help the populous feel safer as well, since many of them served."

He straightened, watching me. Judging me. "And veterans that trained with weapons in their wars?"

"In time I do not see an issue with granting them that which they are familiar with."

Ûlfin bowed slightly, we had reached the office door. The men who had been trailing me took up post to either side. A large tome rested on the desk near the sealed letter. I picked up the letter and placed it in the Orcs large hands.

"I hope I'm not making a mistake."

He shook his head. "No, the troops will be glad for this. It is a needed first step."

"Even if other countries see it as an act of war?"

Ûlfin stuck his head out the door and asked one of the guards to have Brock send me "The Black File" and to leave it on my desk. His blue eyes turned back to me, deep and knowing as the depths of the ocean. "That file will describe some information you need to know. There will be countries that see this as a call to war, aye, but there are others that can and will be allies. Patience, young Lord. Fixing mistakes from those before you cannot be done overnight."

EIGHT

The Book of Procedure was long and tedious, though not as much so as many of the medical books now sitting on the shelves behind me.

Sir Snowball showed himself enough to huddle under my desk, near me but still out of site of the masses moving about this bottom floor of the Penthouse atop the Red Pagoda. It was a comfort to have him besides me, tight against my leg as he watched the world from under the safety the tall desk provided.

I groaned inwardly, going over once again the sections on how to treat Bisnian Royalty.

"How did Father ever memorize all of this?" I asked the cat, knowing I wasn't going to get a response. "Banners featuring both Bisney's arms AND our own need to be on display, we can't offer certain foods, but we need to offer the finest alcohol." I rested my forehead on the pages before me. It was all overwhelming to say the least.

Brock had apparently been at the door when I started lamenting to my cat, and cleared his throat, now standing on one of the chairs I had brought in so he could see over the desk.

"Yer father never memorized a lick of that book." He said, setting more papers down as I looked up. "That's what he had the rest o' us for."

I sighed as I leaned back in the chair. "I know. I thought I should at least be polite and be aware of the things I absolutely have to do, and what I need to avoid at all costs."

"Good." He crossed his arms under his beard, making the red hair shimmering here and there with beads puff out like the chest of a

Paradise Bird. "Yer father never seemed ta care, how the King came into an alliance with him I am not certain."

"Threats perhaps." I shrugged. "Either way we can't ask him, and I wish not to offend King Jean by asking unnecessarily." I glanced at the stack he just set on the desk. "More budgets?"

"Military specific, this time." He said, arms still hidden under the beard. "You've been doing such a good job figuring those out. We've been able to give a couple folk a much needed raise."

I nodded and flipped through the pages quickly, leaning over the book. Mostly charts and spreadsheets. Something else I could delve my attention into and forget the world around me.

Ûlfin came into the room, standing behind Brock and mimicking the Dwarfs' pose, though he lacked the impressive beard. "Lord Bubbles, we still have the assassin to deal with."

Brock looked up to the Orc and back over to me. "He's still alive?"

I looked away, not sure if I should be ashamed or not. "I.... I wasn't sure what to do." I took a deep breath and gathered my wits. "Did he give you any more information?"

Ûlfin shrugged. "He has no family, now that Aeshley, who was his girlfriend, has been executed by King Jean. They were both sent by the High Chieftain, and basically failed since you're still alive." He lifted a hand to his chin in thought. "He's a rather stubborn guy, won't say why he was sent."

"Do we have any magic users on staff?" I looked back at him. "I'm not talking throw around power in battle mages, I'm talking more detail oriented people."

"We have some that specialize in teco-magics, though mages are not fairly common."

Glancing down to the new pile of folders I sighed deeply. "Has there been any word from High Chieftain of Paryda?"

"No."

"That settles it then." I stood up. "Take me to the prisoner."

Ûlfin looked shocked. "But.... Stan..." He started protesting.

I walked around the desk. "He's in chains, there's guards, and the reports I've read in regards to him have failed to mention any magical talent."

The Orc and the two guards took step behind me as I left the office. I motioned for Ûlfin to take the lead.

"Why?" He asked over his shoulder.

"Our physician on staff lacks magical talent. No one else who is aware of how a body functions has any magical talent." He opened the door to the stairwell, one of the guards took it and I followed him through. "I do."

"Lord," He started, using the formal title around others, "are you sure you could torture someone?"

I gritted my teeth. No, I wasn't sure. I doubted I could harm an insect that annoyed me. However, this man did kill my family. He murdered children. Something had to be done.

Silence hung in the air as we descended the flight of stairs from the top of the Red Pagoda to the basement levels. No one spoke, though we were all wondering when the elevators would be repaired. I should have had a team focus on that before the Royal visit. No matter, I could get a runner to send orders once I was finished with this business.

I steeled my emotions in the silence, the way I would before I would tell a patient that the tumor she came to the ER with was cancerous. Before I would leave triage to tell sobbing families that their loved one was no more. If I cut off all emotion, maybe I could get through the next few hours.

I paused before the door, remembering what this man did, what I was about to do. At my nod, Ûlfin unlocked the magi-lock and pushed it open.

The anteroom to the dungeons was filled with guards and lined with walls of computer screens. One large screen was set into the center of each display hub, more than likely meant to take direct video calls, and lines of glowing keyboards beneath those. There was a raised platform in the center, featuring a lone chair and drains around the base.

"Get him in that chair." I growled, fury and anger reaching through the emotionless wall into my voice.

Guards jumped to action, four leaving together in formation into a hallway of cells. Glancing over the displays on that wall I watched them go down the hall and enter a cell, the only one in the hallway holding a prisoner, and escort the man out and down the hall from which they came.

Turning my head from the screens I watched the door, suddenly aware that instead of wearing the typical robes of my father I was wearing slacks and a t-shirt. I almost chuckled, instead shaking my head and steeling my emotions tighter. For some reason a habit of old was having issues coming into being for me at this time.

The man who killed my family was a small Orc, dark green in color so that he appeared almost black, large tusks shining against his deep complexion. He was wearing prisoners clothing, cheaply made fabrics painted in a bright coloration. Ûlfin growled slightly upon seeing him. I stood in my place and watched as he was tied to the chair. He didn't fight. Blood stained his clothing in large swathes, scars standing out bright silver and fresh cuts blazing red and swelling.

Once he was secured the guards stepped aside and left the platform. I waited a moment, watching the man before me as he sagged in his chair.

Then, slowly, I stepped forward and up, reaching out with my aura to feel his. Martin Broadshoulder did not jump at the magical contact, signaling no magical ability.

"Broadshoulder," I said, his head shifting ever so slightly so that his softly pointed ear went to my direction, "that's your name, isn't it?" I walked around before him. He did not look up, yet he kept his attention on me. "Yet you look a little skinny to have such a name."

A soft growl came from him, but no other response. He still had fight in him was the message. I walked behind him, my hand hovering over the space between the mans shoulders, touching his aura directly but not him.

I closed my eyes and paused, taking a deep breath and catching some regret, some hesitation, as to what I had to do.

"Speak," Iron coming into my voice, "and tell me why you were sent."

"To kill you." He growled low.

"So you know who I am."

He snorted. "Educated guess."

I read his aura through the exchange. Dark malice simmered beneath my hand, though the only outlet for it was my family, as if we had personally wronged him.

"Why kill me?" I asked, "What did I ever do to you, a man I never met before now?"

"Orders."

"From the High Chieftan."

"Ukzahg want you dead."

"Again, why?" Irritation was hard to keep out of my voice. His aura, evil as it felt, had not shifted under any lies or other deceit.

"He no tell." No shift. This Orc did not know, he was following orders.

"Any guesses? I assume you would be close to the High Chieftain, being a trusted assassin."

Silence.

"Look," I started, adding compassion from my aura into his, trying to sway his heart and mind, "if you can help me figure out why the High Chieftain, of whom I have only spoken up with reverence, wishes for my death, then I am of a mind to allow you to keep your life."

His aura worked to overpower mine, even without him actively resisting my magic. "Lies."

"Lord." Another voice said, smaller and seemingly far away. I realized I was holding my breath.

I inhaled and looked up, breaking contact from the aura of the assassin before me. "Yes?"

It was a Gnome, a redcap in specific, who spoke up. "Incoming call from Paryda. I believe it's he High Chieftain."

I glanced over at the tied up Orc and stepped up to the front of the platform. "Put him on." If Ukzahg was not immediately angered at interrupting the interrogation of his assassin then surely the fact that I was not dressed to appear before a dignitary would.

In either case I did not find myself caring much for what this Orc thought of me. He wanted my death, I would not bow to such a man.

Ukzahg, High Chieftain of Paryda, was a towering Orc, even larger than Ûlfin by a significant amount, or at least he appeared so on screen. His skin was pale, though had a red tinge, and one of his tusks was broken. Scars lined his face, splitting across his nose and one, pale, eye. He wore furs, and fine armors beneath.

This was a man who had fought his way to the top of the food chain. Paryda was ruled by those who won in combat. Ukzahg was a killer, and had killed the High Chieftain before him with his bare hands, or so the rumors claimed.

I spoke first, abandoning what was considered common courtesy. Both our countries were minor, smaller than others such as Bisney, though Paryda was notably larger than Farysha. Honor dictated that I allow Ukzahg the first word, but he had already angered me, so it was my turn to show him my anger.

"The man who desires me dead," I started, nodding my head in acknowledgment, "High Chieftain Ukzahg of Paryda."

"The runt that ran and hid." The massive Orc growled, his voice like gravel in a childs rock tumbler.

I chuckled, fear of this man deep in my chest and hoping it wasn't surfacing. "The runt that was to inherit nothing yet took over all." I corrected.

"Perhaps..." Ukzahg trailed off. "In any case, a human barely worth my time."

"Yet you called me." I pointed out. "I must be worth enough of your time else that would not have happened." I jabbed a thumb over my shoulder at the Orc tied to the chair. "So must he, else you would not have spent time and effort in his training."

Something flickered in his eyes, some deep emotion that was there for a moment then gone. "He was meant for death when he accepted his mission."

"Yet here he is. Alive, and mostly well." I held my hands out to either side of me. "Though he has been unable to answer some questions I thought quite simple." My heart was racing in my chest, years of training being the only thing keeping me calm.

"And what question is that?"

"Why kill my family? An old man and innocent children." I crossed my arms and did my best to scowl. It must not have been very impressive.

"Because, your father killed my family." His scowl deepened, however that was possible. Ûlfins' eyes snapped up, his brow deepened in a scowl.

I noted the reaction, but kept my attention on Ukzahg. "Oh? I was unaware of such atrocities."

"So you claim."

"I lived most of my life away from my family, training to be a doctor. I wished not this life."

He looked at me for a moment. "Yet it is now yours, as are the sins of your fathers."

I sighed, resting my face within my hand. "So you want to kill me because of something my father did." Anger seeped into my voice. "You had children murdered. One of them was not even of one year." I looked up, tears stinging the corners of my eyes. "An infant, that you had murdered."

He glanced at Martin, then down for a moment. "It was.... Needed."

"Needed?" I walked back over to the restrained Orc. "Is that why you called? To tell me of how you NEEDED to kill CHILDREN?"

"No." His voice was low and even in his grating timber. "I called to announce war."

"War?" I raised an eyebrow., turning my back to Martin and watching the main screen.

"Yes, war. You have thusly armed your forces following my attack. All accords dictate that I need alert you that I will destroy you."

"Even if it costs you your son?" I asked.

Surprise and fury danced over his face. "No one knows..."

"No one KNEW." I corrected, ensuring I was close enough to the captured Orc to affect his aura. "Your facial structure is similar, despite color which I'm assuming his mother was more of a Green Orc of the forests." I ran my hand through his aura again, this time needing to make a show to prevent untold amounts of death.

Seeking nerve clusters, I simply put pressure on them. Martin screamed in sudden pain. Yet it appeared like I never laid a hand on him. I let up pressure after a moment.

"I give you one chance," I started, looking back at Ukzahg, "call off the war, and you can have him back alive."

"If I don't?"

I shrugged, more pressure causing the Orc to scream and twist in his binds.

"I have a few options. He could never walk again as one, nor even raise his arms requiring many to wait on him and return him to you as such." I walked around to his other side, periodically applying and removing pressure. Sweat beaded on the dark Orcs forehead, this was something he had not trained for.

"I could make him walk the Dark Path, laden with threats and molten lava, unarmed and blinded. I assume that is the path he took into Farysha in the first place, being too dangerous to keep under guard."

I came back around to the front, facing Ukzahg but keeping close enough to his son to be able to continue pressure on his nerve endings as necessary.

"Of course, I could also kill him. Though I have not yet decided if I should return his remains nor if you deserve such an honorable motion." I had the High Chieftains' full attention. "The choice is yours."

The answer was long in coming. "How could I trust a Bubbles?"

I shrugged. "I know my family hasn't done much to earn trust, so it is not something I can give an answer to."

"Then I cannot change my decision."

"Even if your son dies because of it?"

He winced. He did care, even if he did not wish to show it. "I have more sons that have not failed me."

I clenched my teeth, acutely aware of my connection to his son's aura. Martins' aura did not showcase sadness nor fear. Instead it felt as if he was....

I spun, the dark Orc having freed himself from half of his binds while the whole room was watching the screens instead. From the corner of my eye I saw Ukzahg smile.

I ducked under his arms, taking a punch to the side, and focused on his aura. I already had a grip on his nerve endings. A single quick thought, a single quick force of will faster than one could blink, and Martin stood in place, frozen by his own body, legs still bound to the chair.

It took me but a moment to redirect my focus from his nerves to his bloodstream, and from there, his heart. Gritting my teeth and feeling his own brain taking back over his nerves to move I started applying pressure.

Instead of slowly beginning to move fluidly, he stumbled, grasping at his chest. I kept up the pressure, increasing it as much as I could.

Suddenly, his aura faded.

Martin Broadshoulder, son of Ukzahg, High Chieftain of Paryda, fell to the floor by my feet, his ties to the chair causing his legs to bend at an odd angle.

Emotions tried to well through me. I kept them down. I had to. This wasn't the first body I've seen. Not the first person to die before me.

Though it was the first time that it was my by hands.

I took a deep breath and opened my eyes, looking back up to the screen, ignoring the wide eyes around me.

"High Chieftain?" I asked.

"See you on the battlefield." He growled before the screens went dark.

NINE

I stood, staring blankly at the dark screen. I wrinkled my nose at the sudden smell from the body at my feet. One thing about death that most seem to ignore is how the body relieves itself once the soul is gone. The smell of fecal matter and urine filled the silent room.

No one moved, everyone was either watching me, or watching the screen the High Chieftain was just on. I cleared my throat. "How long is this dead body going to remain here?"

Men jumped to attention, moving swiftly to untie him from the chairs and move him from the room.

"Make sure the body is sent home." I muttered, approaching Ûlfin. He barked orders, louder than I thought I could speak at the moment. Nausea threatened to overwhelm me. I must have visibly paled as Ûlfin ushered me out of the room.

I vomited into the first trash can I came across. The large Orc said nothing, nor did the guards flanking us. My chest and throat ached as my breakfast emptied into the can. There was an odd pain in my side where his punch had landed.

I killed a man.

It was self defense. He was trying to kill me with his bare hands, stronger than mine own. But I had killed him. I was trying to prevent war, so send him home alive.

"Where did I mess up?" I asked aloud.

Ûlfin placed his hand on my shoulder. It felt warm, comforting. "You were put into a corner. I'll be investigating the men who tied him down. He shouldn't have gotten loose."

I glanced over my shoulder, fearing to move more than so. "You think this was planned?"

"Makes sense. How else would the High Chieftain know to call as soon as you were in to interrogate Martin?"

"Who gave you the information that he had no family?"

A dark glint came into Ûlfins' eyes. "Exactly one of the men who tied him to the chair....."

"Have him arrested for treason." I growled. "Get more information out of him."

The Orc nodded and went back into the room.

I tried to straighten, but failed. Instead I stumbled over, falling towards the floor, head swimming. One of the guards, a man named Hans, caught me, and helped me lean against the cool wall.

"You ok, Sir?" He asked.

I sat for a moment, relishing the chill of the wall. Slowly I nodded. "I will be. Thank you, Hans." Though to be honest the world was still spinning rather ferociously.

He looked vaguely confused, but also worried. "I'm actually glad you're alright, sir." He said sheepishly. "You make working for you easy."

I put my hand on his shoulder. "I try." I smiled weakly. "I know how hard things used to be, so I want to be different."

Hans remained knelt by my side. "It has barely been two days, yet all of us who have worked directly with you have seen the changes. Give it time, the others will as well."

I rested my forehead against my knees. "I was hoping I could start with the whole killing people thing..." My voice trailed off.

He shrugged. "It was our job to protect you, yet we let you up there alone and everyone let themselves be distracted." His eyes found the door we came from. "And everyone saw you defend yourself without needing to move much."

I winced, I could still feel the hit Martin landed on me. Had he hit me in the temple or base of my skull he would have succeeded in his mission. "And get hit in doing so."

Hans' eyes snapped back to me. "You hurt, sir?"

I stretched a little, stretching my aura inwardly. "A couple broken ribs. I'll have to take it easy for a little bit."

My eyes trailed back to the door, my stomach turning. My guards noticed this and shared a look of pity with each other.

"It's not easy, taking a life." Fitz, the man still standing, muttered down in my general direction. "Especially the first time."

I nodded, closing my eyes as my adrenaline continued to crash. The pain of my broken ribs came into acute being in my side, sending bolts up into my brain. My heart refused to calm down, racing as fast as it could.

Still the world spun in circles.

"Lord Bubbles!" I heard Hans shout as the floor rushed up to meet me.

"I'll be fine..." I slurred. I could feel darkness trying to take over my vision and my head. "Keep talking." I focused on Hans' voice.

"Talk about what?" He stammered. "Anything? Uuhhhhh...." I heard rustling.

I strained to listen to anything, to keep my mind grounded and to avoid falling into the darkness.

"Fitz," Hans continued, "has Ûlfin completed his orders?"

"Not yet." Fitzs' voice was a slightly higher pitch than Hans. "I'll get him, I am certain others can take care of it."

"Don't worry, Sir." I felt a hand on my shoulder. "I'm here, and soon Ûlfin will be too."

My breathing calmed, and the threatening black faded back. "Thank you, Hans, and Fitz when he returns." I whispered, fearing to speak more. "Need Vycin for the pain."

He pushed me back down as I tried to sit up. "We can get Doctor Shemayl to get you a prescription."

I laughed, it hurt but I could not stop it from bubbling up out of my chest. "How about I just write one for myself?"

Hans laughed as well, though far more nervously than my own manic chuckles. "I suppose you can do that too."

"What happened?" Ûlfins' voice growled from somewhere just out of sight.

"Didn't Fitz say?" Hans turned to look at him. "Lord Bubbles fainted."

I waved my hand meekly. "Adrenaline crash coupled with the pain of the broken ribs." Again I tried to sit up but was pushed back down. "I'll be fine."

The pale Orc came into my line of sight. "And the fact that you're still grieving and killed a man for the first time has nothing to do with this?"

I looked away. "Right now.... no. Once I've had some medication for the pain....." I couldn't bare to look at anything or anyone other than the floor on which I lay. The cool tiles with intricate patterns one could only see when right upon them. Standing, the detailed filigree vines would only appear as white on white.

Ûlfin sighed as he knelt besides Hans and myself. I glanced over, noting Fitz had returned, back to us as he kept an eye down the hallway. "Can you walk?"

"I will be slow, but yes."

"Should have waited until after the royal visit." The words came as a tight growl from behind his tusks.

"Couldn't." I finally got Hans to allow me to sit up. "Had to be done." He shook his balding head.

I took a calming breath to try and steady my racing heart. "I needed to know why he wanted my family dead. Why he wanted me dead."

"Because your father killed his family?"

"Or at least that he believes as such." I took an offered hand and wobbled to my feet. "I do believe my father capable of such an act, however, Paryda is generally war torn between the various clans within the countries borders." I leaned heavily against Hans. "It would be rather easy for another clan to have killed his family and just blame the most evil man...." I trailed off, looking away, unable to finish the sentence.

They understood. They were there when my father would kill someone who brought him news he didn't like in the most horrifying manners. And that was just over a minor inconvenience.

But he was still my father.

I made a lunge for the trash can again, heaving. Fitz already had it on hand for me to continue to empty my stomach contents.

"I think it's time for you to rest." Ûlfin stated, worry in those blue eyes. "You have been working too much."

"Not working enough..." I muttered, not looking up for a moment. "Let's go."

I started leading the way back up the steps, but faltered and leaned on Hans for support. He was careful in regards to my injured ribs. Fitz ran ahead to ensure the way was cleared and that I had some medication waiting for me when we arrived at the Penthouse.

"And make sure there's someone working on the elevator!" I called up after him as his footsteps echoed.

Slowly our little group worked our way back up the steps. A few times we passed someone, and at others assistants came down to see if I'd like them to grab a gurney or other way to transport me upstairs with minimal effort on my part.

I turned them all down. If I couldn't do this then why should my military follow me? After all, I did just send them off to war.

I heaved again at the thought of more men dieing, at more death, at my expense. This time nothing came up, though the looks of concerns remained.

"Are you certain that you're fine? That it's just broken ribs?" Ûlfin asked, a wary eye at my side.

I nodded. "Aura magic can read better than x-rays if you know what you're looking for."

He didn't seem convinced, but remained quiet anyway. We continued up the steps in silence.

By the time we reached the Penthouse I was more or less walking on my own. Occasionally I'd think of my family, the man I just killed, or the men about to die to defend me and my stomach would seize up again.

I tried dismissing them at the door, to make my way to my bedroom alone, but no one was having it, especially now that we caught back up to Fitz.

The redhead had shoved some medication, Vycin, into my hands with a glass of water. I happily downed a couple of the pills, continuing my bee-line to my room.

Out of fear or respect people cleared my way.

Well, most everyone. Brock stood in the doorway infront of my office, my bedroom was the last door in this hallway.

"Tryin' ta get yerself killed?" He scowled.

I shrugged. "Seemed a good idea at the time."

Brock snapped, doubling over in laughter. "Let's wait for ya to die until you raised a good kid like you, alright?" He clapped a hand on my thigh.

"Yea, sounds like a plan." I chuckled.

"Go rest, I got the rest of the preparations under my beard."

He tried to pat me on the back as he walked past me, but he's a Dwarf and I received a rather awkward pat on my rear end instead.

I shook my head and went into my room for the first time since I moved in. The crews did exactly as directed, and the room looked fairly similar to how I had it set up back home.

I collapsed on the bed heavily at that thought. My home, where I spent the last decade of my life, was gone. Ûlfin and the two guards watched me like hawks, refusing to take a hint to leave me be. I growled up at them.

"I'm in my own room now, I believe you can stand watch outside."

They shared glances at each other and myself before stiffly bowing and excusing themselves.

I watched them go, at first anger flaring in me. I wasn't necessarily certain where it came from, but I had my theories.

First I was still grieving, and would be for some time. Anger was naturally a part of that process. Second was war had just been declared on us. It hasn't even been two days. I haven't lit any of the funeral pyres. Yet another nation decided I was a threat, that I had to be destroyed.

I gritted my teeth, the all too familiar feeling of tears streaming down my cheeks. I hardened my resolve. I would destroy Ukzahg.

Sir Snowball jumped on my bed, startling me. I spun around, wincing and grasping my side as I fell over onto the bed.

"You didn't have to scare me." I squeaked out, barely a whisper.

He meowed in response, slinking over to me, all puffed up. Poor cat was still scared of our new home.

I scratched his head, relieved that the Vycin was hitting my system already, taking the edge off the pain. I straightened and stood back up, going over to one of my dressers to rummage through the drawers.

"Time for bed, buddy." I said aloud. "We can figure out our problems more in the morning."

I relaxed under my plush sheets, though I could not calm my mind. Still my thoughts flew from me, bouncing from showing me the faces of my deceased family, of my new coworkers, and of my friends at the hospital.

Quickly I reached over and grabbed my phone from the nightstand, hoping for any messages or voicemails.

Nothing.

I'll have to check with Ûlfin in the morning that the message was sent. Though, if it wasn't they would be contacting me to ask where I was...

I threw the phone across the room, causing the batteries to fly out as it hit the wall. With a huff I rolled over, and allowed the tears to flow freely.

Sir Snowball curled up on as much of my chest as he could. The good boy always knew when I was upset, though now he half rested on my ribs.

I couldn't bring myself to care.

His purring lulled me into sleep, where the tears and my own mind would have had me stay up all night.

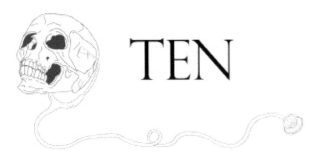

TEN

Nightmares haunted my dreams, now that I was able to sleep, albeit medicated.

I was walking along the street to my office. Well, my old office. Though I wasn't Lord Bubbles anymore, just Doctor Stan.

Yet, everyone avoided me.

No one on the busy street pushed up against me to walk past. No one ducked their head and tried to skirt around me.

Instead every single person avoided me as if I were a sickly dragon, going as far as running out in traffic to get to the other side of the street to avoid me.

A few people had even gotten hit, but when I approached to tend to their injuries others pulled them away.

Finally I arrived to the hospital, but everyone glared at me, whispered behind my back.

"*It's him.*" They were saying. "*HE'S back.*"

"*What, the Pagoda wasn't good enough for him?*"

"*Now he has to return and lord over us here?*"

"*Well, I don't want to work with him, you do it!*"

Hope, Sera, Frayda, everyone I once called friend was glaring at me, watching me as if I were but an old tiger walking into a pen of rabbits.

No one turned their backs to me, and more had gotten hurt.

Quietly I made my way to my office.

Martin Broadshoulder was sitting in my chair, laughing.

* * *

I woke up in a sweat, gasping in pain as my side erupted in a spasm of pain. Hissing in a breath I rolled over, slapping my hand at my nightstand for my medication and water.

A knock on my door irritated me. "Hold. On." I gasped.

Finally I managed to reach the small, orange pill bottle and a squirt bottle of water. After popping a couple pills in my mouth, following with water, I stayed a moment to catch my breath while that knocking continued.

After a few moments in which my cat chose to bolt up and hide under my bed, I stood, holding one arm against my side still blazing in pain.

I walked to the door completely normal, not stumbling and leaning on any piece of furniture nearby to help balance my still half asleep self on my way to the door. However, I probably did look like I was completely insane as I opened the heavy wood door, rubbing sleep out of my eyes which were more than likely puffy from these past few days of tears at night.

Ûlfin stood outside the door.

"Don't you ever sleep?" I grumbled.

He laughed. "When you do. We have guards that take shifts. Even for me." He sighed, his face regaining seriousness. "Get dressed, the best robes. Now."

"Giving orders now?" I jabbed wryly.

"No, just a suggestion to someone who has no idea what he's doing and hasn't actually screwed up yet." He lowered himself to look me in the eye at my level. "You have an hour before King Jean arrives. You need to be presentable."

My mind went blank. Honest to the Gods blank. My mouth must have been hanging open for a while as well.

Ûlfin, with one large finger on my chin, pushed my jaws back closed. "If you can't find a robe that fits where your best suit, the pyres are today as well. Everything is prepared and ready."

My stomach sank into a deep pit. I sagged, leaning against the door, my arm pressing against my injury. Everything I was doing, I did to try to avoid this very topic. This very day.

"Shall I have the chef informed that you will not be eating breakfast today?" He asked, looking around for a servant.

"Maybe just some simple crackers?"

"I can do that." The Orc nodded. "Do you need help getting dressed?"

My eyebrows met in a small burst of anger. I caught my temper and tried to cool it.

"I got into my pajamas just fine, give me a moment for the meds to kick in and I can get into something nicer."

Ûlfin nodded. "You going to do something about your face?"

"Calling me ugly now?" I knew he meant my puffy eyes and the bags underneath, but I couldn't keep the quip in.

He scratched the back of his head. "No, sir, that's not what I meant..."

Reaching up I placed a hand on his shoulder. "I know what you meant, Ûlfin, don't worry." I pulled my hand away. "I'm not sure what can be done. At least for the puffiness right now."

I turned back into the bedroom. "Let's start with me closing the door and changing."

"I can agree with that." The Orc took a step back. "Brock has everything well in hand. Banners hung, meals being prepared. Take the day to entertain your guests. You need a break."

Glancing over my shoulder I shook my head. "I need to go over that Black File you had Brock send to my desk."

He shook his head. "Tomorrow, or tonight once the King and retinue have retired. It's filed away, no one will bother it. For now you need to worry about King Jean."

"Fine." I grumbled through gritted teeth. I needed to know what was in that folder, if it was something that could help in this war.

I spun around, wincing. "Ûlfin, has there been any attacks yet?"

He bowed his head. "A couple ambushes, we couldn't get word out in time. He attacked as soon as he called you."

"Casualties?"

"One hundred fifty nine injured, twenty seven deceased." He whispered. I noted he had the numbers memorized, it was a sign that he cared about the men and women keeping our country safe.

However, it was more death. More death that settled on my shoulders. More death that was mine to carry the blame.

Ûlfin hadn't moved from the door, watching me with a soft expression on his face.

I sagged onto my bench, resting my face in my hands, a position that has become a new norm for me.

Something glinted on the dresser before me, reflecting off the mirror. "Ûlfin," I asked, looking up, "what's this? I don't recognize it."

Ûlfin came in the room and followed my gaze. "It's an old Collar of Estate. Your family stopped wearing it before my time. Alyxa found it in storage, she helped coordinate the shift in decor, and she knew you had quite a few historical items. She thought you might prefer it on display here, rather than hidden in a box in the shadows."

I stood, leaning against the dresser with one arm, tracing the inlayed gold with my other hand. The chain itself was cast into the heads of dragons, eyes inset with volcanic glass, intertwined around each other. Either end of the chain hooked to a simple golden shield, enameled with the Coat of Arms of Farysha in full color: white, a black chevron issuing from the base, and overall a sleeping golden dragon.

"I thought the dragon was red on the arms." I noted aloud.

Ûlfin looked over at it. "Perhaps it's meant to signify the leadership?" He suggested. "Or, maybe, it once was golden?"

"Maybe." I stared at it a moment. "Oh, you did get the message to my office, right?"

"Yes, I went myself before you woke and gathered your items." His eyes moved back to me from the amulet on the Collar. "I was certain you'd have noticed the items in your new office."

"I thought as much, I just..."

"You were just hoping to hear back from any of them and haven't yet?" He finished the sentence.

I didn't answer. I moved to the closet and started digging through the robes of state Father always wore. Half closing the door to the immense closet I tugged off my pajamas, wincing at the pain in my side, only made lesser by the medication and not completely gone.

Finally, in the light, I glanced down at the injury itself. It was swollen, and a sickly indigo color, pale yellow around the area. I had seen worse, but the bruising around broken bones was never fun to look at.

Turning back to the rack of robes I started tugging one on. It was black with silver and gold trim embroidered on. A golden belt cinched it shut. I walked out into my bedroom feeling like I was wearing a bedsheet.

Ûlfin burst out laughing the moment he saw me. I couldn't help it, I smiled and started laughing too.

The robes were probably a five extra large size, I was just a large. I sagged my shoulders, causing part of the robes to fall down, revealing my bare skin underneath.

"You know, I have tailored business suits. I'm just going to shower and wear one of those." I admitted in defeat.

"Shall we have the robes taken in for you?" Ûlfin asked, standing up.

I shook my head. "No, I don't think I'll wear them." I glanced in the mirror at myself. "Yea, I'm a mage, but robes have never been *me*."

"I get it." Ûlfin was still smiling. "I will go oversee that security is ready for His Majesty." He half bowed at the waist. "I will meet you in the entry chamber."

I dipped my head in response. "Of course. Thank you, Ûlfin."

The Orc left as I turned to the other door in my bedroom, the master bathroom.

I had never actually been in the master bath, we used the more public restrooms with the rest of the staff. I took a moment to look around.

The lavishes of the bedroom had continued into the bathroom. There was a small chandelier for some reason, marble his and hers sinks rimmed in gold with a dark, slate counter. One side had a standing waterfall shower made to look natural, complete with low light vines and plants, separated from the toilet with a rocky wall. The other side had a large soaker tub inset into a boulder of a geode, its' violet gems shimmering in the light.

Purple and indigo flowers scattered throughout the room in golden pots tied everything together. It might have been tacky, but it didn't look that horrible.

"Well then." I muttered aloud, letting the robes fall to the ground and setting the belt on the counter before entering the shower.

The waterfall shower felt nicer than any shower I had ever remembered. The stone floor helped smooth and relax my feet, and the soaps, though apparently labeled such as Dragon's Blood, had a warm smell that reminded me of a little bakery near Hykur Memorial.

I thought I was out of tears.

I slid down the rocky wall of the shower, gaining some cuts to match my bruised and broken side, across my back. I leaned there, curled up, sobbing quietly.

How could I ever have thought that they would still *want* to talk to me. I lied to them for a decade. I'm now the man who everyone was taught to fear. To leave alone.

I mourned my old life. I mourned lost friends. I mourned lost family. And at the same time I was angry at them. At myself. Here I was, the Lord of Farysha, curled up in pain and grief in my shower.

ELEVEN

I found a black suit that I hadn't worn in about a year when a coworker was killed after a patient came in high on a deadly drug mixture. He took out three guards as well before he was subdued.

Though I still felt sadness over the incident, I was one room over that night, I had time to process that night.

It has barely been three days since I lost my family, I thought I had run out of tears, but I knew more would come. For now, I needed to focus on work, that helped me cope.

I watched myself in the mirror. My usually sharp features baggy and puffy. Shorter dark hair untamable and stuck in different directions, still damp.

I had shaved, a few pink and red marks across my cheeks and chin oddly matched the pink around my eyes. I took a shaky breath and again ran my fingers over the Collar of Estate before me.

I didn't have time to stand there, just looking at my pathetic self.

Slowly, gently, I picked up the golden links and slid it over my head.

The chain was not backed by any fabrics, something I've seen with lesser offices. Instead it was simply gold with obsidian glinting in the surface. The amulet, the Coat of Arms of Farysha with a golden dragon, sat between the points of my collarbone.

It was heavy, but moreso that it should have been. I knew a large part of that weight was only in my head. Instead of a crown, I had this. I felt the weight of those that depend on me to keep them safe. To keep them alive.

The weight of those souls already lost defending me.

Gods, it hasn't even been three days.

I gritted my teeth and tried to clear my thoughts. *We don't have time for me to sit here feeling sorry for myself while King Jean waits on me.* I thought.

I smoothed my jacket and left my quiet room for the bustling commotion of the Penthouse. Ûlfin was waiting for me, a package in hand.

"The Royal caravan is almost to the Pagoda." He informed me. "The elevators are still out, though being very obviously worked on, so you have some more time if you wanted to eat breakfast."

I shook my head. "No, call it nerves but I don't think I'll be able to stomach much right now."

His gaze grew distant for a moment. "Me either." He whispered.

"This isn't the first assassination you've seen." I pointed out. "You've been here for three generations."

Ûlfin looked away, I thought his color paled even more than it had with his age. "Never before were children targeted." He said through gritted teeth.

Together we stood in silence, looking away from each other at everyone skirting around. Finishing up decorations, displaying the Royal Arms of Bisney, a fierce golden lion, crowned in silver, upon an intricate pattern of blues, alongside our own Arms with the red sleeping dragon. At the same time, those that need not be here began to clear out. Any extra servants and assistants Brock brought in to help with the change of leadership were given paid vacation. They would be going to spend time with their families, or at a resort down by one of our beaches.

I needed to distract myself. I nodded to the package in the Orcs large hands. "What's in the box?"

"Oh!" He suddenly spun around, causing me to flinch slightly. "Sorry, it's something for you. Again it's something we found in storage from at least two or three centuries ago."

Ûlfin handed the box to me. "We had to get some of the leather treated, and some more replaced." He shrugged. "We also felt like we needed to add a holster for your sidearm, we are living in a more modern world." I opened the box to reveal a simple sword in an old, elegant sheath. The Arms of Farysha tooled into the leather, highlighted with gold leaf. The belt was simple and white, holding a drop holster on the side opposite the blade, again featuring the Faryshan Arms.

Sliding the belt around my waist, shifting my coat so as to not look awkward, I sent a runner to fetch my pistol from my briefcase. As I waited I bent over and clipped a strap from the holster around my upper leg, tightening it so it wouldn't flop about but not so tight to turn the strap into a tourniquet. They promptly returned, and the weapon clicked into place, a protective strap clicking up to keep the pistol secure. I practiced pushing the strap aside and half pulling the pistol up a few times, adjusting where needed, before I felt comfortable in the belt setup.

"Thank you, Ûlfin, and be sure to pass my thanks to everyone who assisted in repairs and additions." I rolled my shoulders, looking around the quickly clearing hall. "I do hope that I do not offend the King."

"I doubt you will." The Orc watched the stairwell doors. "We are, after all, in a time of war."

"How many more since yesterday?" We both knew I didn't have to specify.

Ûlfin sighed heavily. "In the guard, another two hundred and six injured, forty three dead. In the military itself, now that they have joined the fight, I do not have the totals for. Brock might, High General Ahun will for sure." He glanced at me through the corner of his eye, his head barely moving. "Let us not fret about it for now. You concern yourself with the King and today."

"It's hard not to." I kept my eyes trained on the stairwell. "These men are dead or hurt because they were defending me."

I saw Ûlfins' jaw tighten, but he didn't say anything.

We resigned ourselves to standing in silence, each resting an arm on a weapon. I could feel my ribs ache with every breath, but I was learning to push away the pain, let the medicine do its' job. Even still, I should be on bed rest for at minimum a week to allow my ribs to heal right. Alas, I did not have the time for such matters.

I simply strengthened my aura around my ribs to hold them in place while I was up and moving around. It helped numb the pain a little as well.

King Jean Lision did not come out of the stairwell first. Instead, two men in black uniforms, both Elven and not sporting obvious weapons, came through and scanned the room, speaking into microphones in their ears.

"Here we go." Ûlfin whispered under his breath. I nodded slightly to him in response.

The hall was clear, save for us in a doorway and the two guards. We didn't relax as they approached us.

"Lord Bubbles?" One asked.

"The one and only." I responded.

They glanced over our weapons before speaking to their earpieces again. "All clear, two in hall, Lord Bubbles and Bodyguard."

Ûlfin glared slightly at the man who had spoken. "Head of the Farysha Guard and Security of the Red Pagoda."

The man who spoke seemed to ignore the correction.

I looked back over my shoulder down the hall, a half-Elf and a Human waited in freshly polished armor, sword and pistols at hips, looking deadly serious. Aelyr and Kutz, my guards for the day. They both heard the exchange and were fighting to keep a serious face for when they were needed to follow up as my retinue.

One of them whispered something into the doorway they were standing by, more than likely to Brock who would also take up a place in my retinue in short order.

I shook my head ever so slightly, hoping they'd understand it as '*Time to be serious, let's save the jokes for later.*' Though I wasn't certain if they understood, as they were still sporting goofy grins.

I'll let Brock or Ûlfin scold them later. For now, I had more important matters to attend to.

King Jean was human, though a subtle point to his ears and a golden ring around his green irises told of some Elvish blood in his lineage. His hair was a pale gold, akin to sand on a beach. He was tall and well built, wearing a simple golden crown bearing lions and sapphires, and a deep blue suit that I had assumed was black until the shades caught in the light.

A young lady was with him, following just behind. Her hair was slightly darker, though her blue eyes also were rimmed with gold and her ears rounder than that of her father.

Princess Aleyna of Bisney might have been wearing an elegant cut blue dress and a slight silver circlet, but no make-up touched her face, for it too was bearing the marks of grief.

His Majesty's face, however, was stone cold sober. I thought I saw soft bags under his exotic eyes, however they were hidden well.

He softened as we approached each other, seeing my own sadness evident on my face.

Ûlfin bowed deep at the waist, King Jean's bodyguards mimicking the motion. His Majesty and myself inclined our heads at each other, and I did a short, curt bow towards the Princess in a sign of respect.

"Thank you," He started, "for allowing us to visit in your home."

"We are honored to host you." I replied. "I do apologize for the state of the elevators, there was much damage when..." I trailed off, catching my thoughts and emotions.

His cold face warmed and softened. "I am aware of what happened. You have a most excellent Head of Administration." He took a deep breath, I was amazed he wasn't panting after the climb, and looked around.

"I am also pleased zat you showed true concern, and appear to have a good emotional range."

"Your Majesty?" I asked, hoping for clarification on the matter.

He waved his hand in dismissal. "Thou shalt not speak ill of ze dead on ze day we send zem to their peace." It felt more like a quote than a statement. "A matter for another time."

I nodded deeply. "As you wish, I will respect your customs."

He smiled, though it did not meet his eyes. "I see you have chosen to change some of yours."

"I did not have ample time to have any robes remade or properly taken in, however, I have always found myself looking rather awkward in such a garment." I gestured down at my attire. "This I am more accustomed to wearing, though the sword and holster are new to me."

King Jean rose an eyebrow. "Ancestral sword?"

"Yes, Your Majesty. It was found in storage while I had the Penthouse and Guest Suites prepared for you and your retinue." I looked around. "I am assuming they are awaiting us in the entry rooms or have been guided to the suites?"

"Zey await us outside." For a moment sadness overtook his features, but just a moment. His face returned to that of relaxed blankness. "We should return downstairs, it is bad luck to be late to say goodbye to loved ones."

My breath caught in my chest. I knew that today was *that* day, but deep down I was hoping to avoid the topic, avoid the whole day. I nodded to Ûlfin who took a step back and moved his hand in a single signal.

At once the two guards and Brock came from the hall, a few assistants in tow that the Dwarf was busy issuing orders to before we left the Penthouse.

The three bowed deeply as they approached, each muttering greetings and condolences. Together, the King to my right and Ûlfin to my left, I led the group downstairs and outside into the morning breeze.

TWELVE

As customs dictated the procession traveled from the Red Pagoda to the Sleeping Volcano in the center of Farysha. It took two hours to reach the summit. Pyres were already set up, and high ranking individuals in the Guard and Military were directing the set up for the pyres and placement for the bodies.

I had requested that all those who fell in battle to defend a war started by a mad Orc who desired me dead be a part of the funeral pyres. Their families already had gathered around the rim of the dormant volcano.

"Zey will expect a speech." King Jean whispered to me as we left our respective cars and made our way to the largest of the pyres.

I looked back to Brock for help. He just shrugged and mouthed, "Yer on yer own lad."

Sure enough there was a platform set aside for us, a small crowd already gathering around. We stopped at the edge of the crowd, both of us hesitating. Brock tugged on the hem of my coat, I leaned over so he cold talk to me without many eavesdroppers.

"Ya won't be lighting the fire, just stay on the platform." He nodded up to Ûlfin who towered over him, "Ya got good people keeping ya safe."

"Thank you, for everything." I said, loud enough that Ûlfin an others could hear me as well.

I didn't check if he did, the crowd was already clearing a path for us, bowing deeply, so we could ascend the steps.

Working in private was one thing, but now I could not pretend that I was still my old self. That Stan had died alongside those we give to the

flames this day. I still will strive to act as I always have, but no longer
could I hope for my far more simple life.

In silence King Jean, Princess Aleyna, and myself took the small steps
to the platform. We could see every stack ready to light, our own loved
ones before us.

Around each body was hay, carrots, and other horse feed so that the
horses that pull the Chariots of the Reapers would not go hungry. On
their eyes were coins to pay the Reapers, so that their souls would not
be punished for crimes.

Deep down I knew that for some of those before me the coins would
do nothing to stay the Reapers' wrath. I almost wished that they hadn't
bothered with the gold for Father.

Other items were in the pyres of others. The children, small bundles
alongside their parents, had their favored toys. I noted almost all of
the soldiers I could see who had fallen had their service weapons, and
photos of loved ones. My father had but a single picture upon his
wrapped breast, a picture of our family when Mother was still alive.

I glanced at Jean besides me. His daughter was barely holding it
together. His jaw was tense, and he only stared in the distance, at
nothing in particular.

Looking downwards, then up and around at the crowd around me
I noted Hope, Sera, and a few others from the office. I pulled my
eyes away from them before I could read their expressions. They were
probably here to see my pain, to laugh upon their return.

That hurt as much as the death surrounding me.

At long last, I spoke into the silence. "I know you are expecting a
speech." I looked back up, looking at the crowd around us, even Jean
had turned his gaze to me.

"I know you expect me to hail the achievements of my father," I lifted
a hand towards His Majesty, though humbled as he was already before
the populous, "of Prince Eryk of Bisney who was wed to my own sister."

I shook my head, slowly. "Alas I did not know the Prince well enough to speak of his memory, my father had pushed me from the family years ago. As such, I have no kind words on his behalf for this day."

My head fell, I couldn't keep looking at the crowd. I gathered my aura tighter around my vocal chords, helping ensure all could hear me. "Today we grieve for more than the lost Royals. Yesterday, Paryda announced war on Farysha. They sent ambushes before I could react and have not relented their attacks."

I took a deep breath and looked back up. "Today we pray for all the souls lost these past three days. Today we remember those taken from us too early, sons, nieces, nephews, soldiers."

I stepped forward, resolve entering my voice. "I did not want this." I spread my arms around me, spinning slowly. "I wanted to live my life as a doctor, to live my life as I so wished. I did not ask for men to fight and die for a man they don't know, for one so unprepared for life in leadership."

My hands clenched into fists by my side. "So today I want each of us to remember those taken from us. Mourn for the soldiers, for the children, for the innocence lost. Mourn for the lives that have changed because of this. Children that will have no father, wives that have lost husbands," I wanted to look at Hope and the others, but I didn't, I couldn't, "and for those who have had their livelihoods uprooted to take the stage and become something they were never meant to be." My voice trailed to almost a whisper, barely audible even with the magical enhancement. "Thank you, everyone, for being here." I finished, turning back around to face the front, to face the bodies of my family.

Not even Jean in all his royal glory was able to keep tears of his face.

We stood together, the three of us, in silent misery as the fires were lit and the volcano took on a macabre life.

After an hour the crowd began to disperse. Within three hours the only ones left were our guards and those who had lost someone dear by their respective pyres.

Suddenly, as the sun was nearing the high point in the sky, the pain of my broken ribs seared through me. With a grunt I fell to a knee, searching my pockets for my medicine and a water bottle.

Neither were there.

As I fell something buzzed by my ear like an angry hornet.

"Get down!" The Dwarf shouted.

Already Brock, Ûlfin, and the Princess were by my side, Jean having been lost deep in trance-like thought.

"Anyone have the Vycin? I seem to have forgot it." I said through gritted teeth.

"No, I thought ya had it." Brock stated, standing over me.

Princess Aleyna, however, looked concerned as her eyes scanned the world around us. "What happened?"

"Broken ribs." Brock answered as Ûlfin swore an oath over my shoulder as he was taking off running. Another angry hornet screamed past my head. "Oh, and someone's shootin' at us."

One of the guards had to tackle Jean to break him of the trance. "What is happening?" He asked, accent heavy.

Brock looked around before answering. "Lord Bubbles left his medication for his broken bones at the Penthouse and the guards found an assassination attempt. Had the Lord not fallen..."

He didn't need to finish the sentence. Had my ribs not suddenly ached there would be a new pyre added to the ring.

"The threat has been disposed of." A deep, rumbling voice said from behind us. We all turned to face the speaker.

"Your Majesty and Your Highness, may I present my High General Ahun Dragonfist."

Ahun Dragonfist, the leader of the Military Forces of Farysha, was a red Orc with blonde hair in a tight cut and two impressive tusks jutting from his lower jaw, one of which was broken with a blazing scar across his cheek. Rather than the more ceremonial armor that my guards had chosen to wear for the day, his gear was more on the tactical side, with maille sticking out from underneath ballistic body armor. A rifle was slung across his chest, a sword and pistol at either hip.

He bowed at the waist in respect to us and straightened. "You are safe now."

"Thank you, High General." I said. Jean, rubbing at his eyes, mirrored my response.

Ahun looked around, at the pyres now smoldering piles. "I would suggest you return to the Penthouse, M'Lord."

I glanced around, first at Ûlfin, Brock, and then at what was left of the fires. I didn't move.

King Jean rolled his shoulders and stood, the stoned face expression returning to his features. "I believe you are right, Master Dragonfist." He held his arm out to his daughter who took it, using it to help stand. Ûlfin offered to help me down the stairs, I shook my head. I had to do this on my own. I had to show that I was stronger than I felt. Once in the safety of the car I could be weak again, though I didn't want to be.

I wondered how many dear friends and family King Jean had sent to the earth to be so dead of expression at the loss of his only son. How much loss he had to suffer.

How much more I would have to suffer to remain so steadfast.

I was grateful when we reached the cars and the driver opened the door for me. Ûlfin chose to sit up front, Aelyr and Kutz choosing to ride in a separate vehicle.

I wished I could have passed out on the way home. I wished that my coworkers hadn't come. I wished that none of this had happened.

Mental wounds re-opened, though there were no more tears to shed. I spent the ride trying to compose myself.

I don't think I succeeded.

THIRTEEN

We sat in silence around the grand table. For once I was in the Head Chair, with King Jean to my right and Princess Aleyna to my left. Hans and Fitz took over for Aelyr and Kutz and stood behind me to either side. Ûlfin was off checking on security and getting reports in from the border.

The feast the chef prepared for us was remarkable, though three of us barely touched our plates.

In silence we poked at our plates rather than eating before King Jean rose and bowed his head towards me. "By your leave I shall like to retire early."

"I think you have a good idea there." I said, nodding. "You, Her Highness, and your guards and retinue have the entire upstairs and Guest Suite a few floors down. Servants are available to lead you to wherever you need to." I stood as well, gathering up my plates. "There are two rooms specifically set aside for you and Princess Aleyna, each are marked with the Royal Arms on the door."

"Thank you, Lord Bubbles." He said. "Aleyna?"

The princess stood, bowed her head towards me, and followed her father and some servants to the stairwell.

I watched them leave before picking up my plates and taking them into the kitchen. In my daze I set them in the sink and turned on the water, falling into the habit of washing what I used.

No one interrupted me, though someone did take the wet dishes from me once they were clean. The process only took a few minutes then I was drying my hands off and wandering towards my office.

Blankly I stared at the big book covering everything I needed to do to appease the various leaders and cultures of the different countries. I picked it up and spun around, placing it on one of the bookshelves in the office.

Heading back to my desk the filing cabinets caught my eye. I pushed my chair over and ran my fingers over the labels. *Private, Administration, Political, Guard Reports, Military Reports, Budget.*

My finger traveled back to private, my aura triggering a magi-lock and the drawer popped open.

Two folders sat inside. First was the cause of death reports to my family. Second was the Black Folder Ûlfin had asked me to go over.

Now was as good a time as ever.

I picked up the folder and returned to my desk, placing the bundle of papers on top. The pages were yellowed with age, these were possibly older than even my grandfather. Some of the pages that had dates on a corner confirmed my suspicion, they were almost two hundred and fifty years old.

Gently I went through the reports, reading how my ancestor started placing groups of people allied with him in countries that voted in their leadership. The orders to these groups were simple, to remain there, have children, and eventually cause enough disturbances that they could get one of their faction elected.

Directions on how to do such were included with these pages. They were to follow them to the letter, and, once the time came that they were to swear loyalty to whoever was the current Lord of Farysha.

That Lord would be me.

Two different countries, Ishta and Akyta, had recently elected leadership that most considered an odd match, but that allied with the beliefs of my own family. They were ready do join in, what my ancestor called, the Empire at a given notice.

"Ûlfin." I called, having questions.

Hans ran and fetched the Orc for me. It took a few minutes before he was before me. He closed the door as he entered the room. I sealed the aura, blocking sound and other magics from coming in.

"You summoned me?" He asked.

I tapped the contents of the folder. "How many others know of this?"

"Myself, Brock, and Ahun." He took a seat in one of the two chairs on the opposite side of me. "I assume your father never read it."

I rested my elbow on the desk, and my chin in the palm of my hand, tapping the Black Folder with my other hand. "I believe that this war Paryda is dragging us into will flame into something larger."

"You think His Majesty will toss in with our lot, sending reinforcements to our forces?" The chair groaned slightly as he leaned back in it, thinking.

"I'm not sure." I said with a sigh. "If he chooses to continue to honor the alliance, then probably, though we need to do more than defeat Ukzahg."

His eyes narrowed as he watched me. "You want to make an example?"

I sat back, waving my hands in dismissal of the thought. "No, no. Well, not exactly." I settled my hands in my lap. "Parydian customs dictate that if someone born in Paryda calls out the High Chieftain in honorable combat that whoever wins claims the highest title of those in the fight."

Ûlfin bowed his head. "Ukzahg is not to be underestimated."

I leaned forward. "Does he realize that my two highest ranking armed forces individuals are both Parydian Orcs?"

"I cannot win against him." He growled.

"And Ahun? I do believe he has been undefeated in the hand to hand combat tournaments that went on behind Fathers' back."

Ûlfin looked away, towards the sealed door. "I will speak to him. Taking over Paryda, basically by force even if the customs permit such a thing, will spark the notice of the rest of the world."

"Yet if we don't Ukzahg will work hard to pummel us to the ground until I am dead and Farysha ashes."

"You would be right."

"Have the High General begin preparations for a more aggressive assault." I stood up, wincing slightly as my ribs protested. "I will not stand by and watch hundreds, nor even thousands, fight for me. Especially if we can end this quickly."

Ûlfin stood as well. "Then I will also start sending messages to Ishta and Akyta, to begin preparations to join in an alliance shall it be necessary."

"Thank you, Ûlfin." I released the spells around the room.

"Are there any other plans for tonight?" He asked as he reached the door.

"No, I think I need to take my rest before I injure my side any further." I returned the Black Folder to its' location in the locked cabinet.

"I didn't think you had world domination in you." Ûlfin joked. "It's been plaguing your family for so long, but you've always been different."

"It's not that." I retorted. "You know that. This is self defense. Besides, if they think that making up who attacked them in order to declare war is acceptable, they need to learn that it's not."

"You would be right on that one." He bowed his head. "Take care, Stan. I'll go inform Ahun on the plan."

"I wish he'd be able to report in himself more often." I grumbled, slamming the cabinet drawer shut and turning to follow Ûlfin out the door.

The Orc laughed. "I do to, messengers can only be trusted so far." He grew serious as I met him outside in the hall, closing the office door behind me. "Though we both understand why he doesn't."

"We're at war." I said, in almost a sigh. "He's needed on the front, I can't possibly ask him to abandon our soldiers."

"I'm off then." He placed a hand on my shoulder, giving it a soft squeeze. "Today was a close call, I think until we understand more of what's going on we should keep you inside."

"Can't argue there." I turned around, looking up at the Orc. "Thank you, again, for your service and loyalty. I know I say it a lot, but I feel like in the past it was never said enough." I put my hand on his on my shoulder and gave it a squeeze in response. "Rest up, the Gods know I'd be dead without you."

Ûlfin gave a sad smile before turning down the hall towards the main room and the stairs. I watched him walk off. At the end of the hall he bowed slightly before he continued on out of my line of sight.

Princess Aleyna stepped into view, wearing but a simple shift of a nightgown. Her sandy hair was let down over her shoulders, and she looked like sleep had been evading her for some time.

I bowed respectfully. "Your Highness, I see sleep is not your friend this night."

She shook her head. "No, nor has it these past few days."

"I understand too well." I put my hand on the office door, near the plate that read "Lord Bubbles" at eye level. "I have been working myself until I pass out, and even then..."

"Even then the nightmares come to haunt you with memories." She finished, looking at the nameplate as well.

I closed my eyes a moment before looking back to the Princess.

"Is there something you needed, Princess?" I asked.

"Company, unless you had something to help sleep."

I smiled warmly and opened the office back up. "I think I can do both."

I let her enter first, leaving the door open behind me.

She took a seat in the chair Ûlfin was just in as I walked around to the shelves on either side of the filing cabinets. They held a mixture of items from books to artifacts to different supplements and medications that might be needed at a moments notice.

I grabbed a bottle off a shelf and took it to Princess Aleyna.

"Melatonin gummies." I explained. "They'll help you fall asleep."
She opened the bottle and we both took some. "How long does it take
to kick in?"
I put the bottle back and sat in the seat opposite her instead of my
normal spot behind the desk. "You should start feeling drowsy within
half an hour to an hour, though it won't fully kick in until you decide
to attempt sleep once again."
"So if you choose to stay awake, you can?"
I laughed awkwardly. "You can, however you might have a nasty
headache in the morning."
She smiled slightly, it was warm and nice to look at. "You sound like
you have learned from experience."
"I spent the last ten years working in the emergency room. I didn't
handle surgeries but I did work with many of the patients that came in."
I leaned forward on my elbows. "There's this law that everyone, unless
it's an emergency, has to be indoors by nightfall. Working third shift
meant we had to stay inside until dawn came." My eyes were glued to
the floor, I never did like working that shift, however, I greatly missed
everyone I worked with.
Seeing them at the funeral, I felt like a fool.
"I'm assuming zat nights were not always peaceful, despite ze curfew."
"Domestic abuse victims came in often. Gang wars as well." I looked at
her, barely moving my head. It was nice, talking about what was. "There
were nights where it would be dead silent, then all of a sudden we'd
have seven gunshot wounds, three stabbings, and a husband that had
been poisoned."
"You don't have to talk about it, if you do not wish to." She muttered
softly.
I found myself enjoying her company, her accent, her just being there,
listening. In the past I could always talk to Hope and Sera, they knew
and were often there, but this felt different somehow, more profound.
Maybe it's because we both said our goodbyes to family today.

"No, it's comforting, talking about it."

"You said you were mourning your old life as well." Her eyes met mine. We held the gaze for a moment before I looked away and nodded.

"I never wanted this. This title, the Penthouse, any of it. I just wanted to be me, even if I had to use a fake name. I had friends who won't even talk to me anymore since they learned the truth."

Aleyna scooted her chair closer and placed a delicate hand on the small of my back. I felt her aura at the touch, flinching slightly at the unexpected touch, the unexpected kindness and warmth of her aura. She jerked her hand quickly away. "My apologies."

"Don't be." I smiled at her. "I'm a mage, I guess I've been caught up in so many darker or focused auras from wo.... From being a doctor to here that the difference of yours shocked me slightly." I looked away, somewhat embarrassed. "It was warm, and nice. I liked it."

We sat in silence for a time, hands on our laps, before I spoke again. "I didn't know your brother that well, I had only met him a couple times. It would be nice if, before you left, we could sit and talk about them?"

"I think zat would be an excellent idea." She responded. "Your sister was.... different, though I did not get to meet much of ze rest of your family."

"Besides maybe my nieces and nephews you weren't missing that much." My voice came out as a whisper.

Again silence came into the air. Neither of us broke into tears, something deep down helped me feel better. Maybe it was just being so close to someone who cared.

Aleyna rose from her chair. "I believe it is time for rest."

I stood as well, extending a hand to her. "I think you're right. It was nice getting to chat, and to have some company."

She smiled as she grasped my hand in a surprisingly firm handshake. "It was. Thank you for ze melatonin, doctor."

My smile faltered and I glanced away. Could I still be called a doctor? I was Lord now, and had killed a man, albeit in self defense.

I returned my gaze to the Princess and gave a tight bow, kissing the back of her hand as custom dictated. "I hope you have a decent nights sleep, free of dreams, Princess."

She was blushing a beautiful rosy color. "You as well, Lord Stan."

She returned down the hall towards the stairs. I went the opposite direction to my own room, feeling a million pounds lighter.

FOURTEEN

I was able to eat breakfast that next morning. His Majesty picked at his plate slightly more than yesterday, and Princess Aleyna ate a healthy amount as well.

King Jean spoke first that morning. "It would appear zat you both have better appetites zis morn."

Aleyna glanced at my direction briefly. "I could not sleep last night, so I wandered. Lord Bubbles offered me companionship, and a way to help sleep." She smiled briefly. "It would seem our discussion help you as well."

I bowed my head curtly. "It did, thank you for the opportunity, Your Highness."

King Jean stared at his plate, lost in thought. Finally he looked up, glancing at one of his advisors.

The advisor, a small girl with raven black hair, watched me for a moment before nodding to the King. Curious, I watched her back, how her eyes didn't exactly flicker at anyone in particular, but rather the space around the person who held her attention.

I dropped my fork and leaned back in sudden realization. "You are an aura-reader."

She dipped her head in a bow. "Yes, Lord Bubbles. I was born with ze gift to See, so zat I may best warn others of impending danger."

I leaned forward onto the table, watching her brown eyes. "I have known two others, when I studied at the University. Would you mind if I gave you a small test, a question really?"

She looked confused but nodded.

"What color is my aura?"

"Gold, with green sparks around your ribcage." She answered with no hesitation.

I relaxed and smiled, the sparks would be my reinforcement of my broken ribs so they could heal as I moved around. "You can indeed See. I am sorry for the test, I needed to be certain."

"I understand, you would hate for a fraud to spread lies." Her tight smile returned. "Though it is nice to see a warm aura around you, your fathers aura..." She looked away with a shudder.

I looked away as well. I knew of the horrors my father committed, many of which right here in the Penthouse. I tried to forget about them, the lesser horrors that I had to witness.

"We shall not speak ill..." King Jean muttered. "Though Katrinah here has spoken highly of your auras activities. It does give me hope for ze future of Farysha."

"Our alliance then, it will continue?"

He nodded. "Yes, however, with ze family ties broken by death I do have a few items of consequence to consider before our departure."

"A new way to seal the alliance?"

He waved his hand in the air. "New, old, either way things as such have been done in the past." He rose, this time his guards and retinue rose as well. "I have decided to go on a tour of Farysha. We will depart shortly and return in a few days once the tour has concluded and I have made my decision."

I stood up, hands on the tables' surface. "Do you wish for me to join you?"

"No," King Jean said softly. "I am aware of the threat against you, and zat you have much to do to secure your title. Such things cannot be done with but three days of work."

Which was right. I have only begun to chip away at the mountain of wrongs that needed to be righted for this country to have any economic success.

I bowed my head at his choice. "As you wish, Your Majesty."

He nodded his n response. "We will take our leave zen, Aleyna."

The Princess took his arm and followed him towards the exit. The elevators were cleared to work this morning, though His Majesty led Her Highness down the steps, allowing his retinue and most of his guard to take the elevator in his stead.

I watched them leave, feeling suddenly alone despite Ûlfin and my other two bodyguards being nearby. The quiet of the grand hall was unnerving.

I went to my office, glanced at the pile of papers, and turned away, leaning against the doorframe. The hallway was returning to its' normal haste, runners dodging each other and waiters bringing food to the servants quarters and to Brock.

I knew I had work to do, but at the moment I wasn't sure that even paperwork could help distract me. Aelyr noticed my expression.

"Sir, you don't have to do paperwork if you don't want to." He suggested.

"Yea," Kutz agreed. "you have been rather pent up lately."

Aelyr gave the other man a punch in the shoulder in jest. "Really, with the puns? Again?"

Kutz laughed at the half-Elf, rubbing his arm where he had been hit. "I thought it was very *punny* of me!"

I couldn't help but break into a smile and a laugh. It felt good. I felt oddly good, despite the ache in my side resulting in a wince.

Kutz smiled his goofy smile. "Nice to see that you're in a better mood today, Sir."

I glanced back down the hallway, towards the main hall and the exits. "Yea, I had good company last night, I think that helped us both significantly."

Aelyr was more serious. "Though it will still take some more time to heal fully. Take it easy, don't overwork yourself."

Ûlfin appeared behind them, having had to check on messages from Akun. "There is still the matter of the assassin from yesterday."

My attention snapped to the Orc. "I was under the assumption that the soldiers had killed him on site."

"They did, however...." He trailed off.

I gritted my teeth and drew my eyebrows together. "Something came up?"

"Something bigger, something deeper, than Paryda."

I ran my hands through my hair, taking a deep breath to calm my rising heart rate. "Let me guess, hidden assassination group within our own borders?"

Ûlfin looked shocked at my guess.

"Ûlfin, it's not so secret down there," I pointed in the general direction of Hykur, "it might not be common for discussion, but everyone knows that the Dragon Talons exist." Realization came into me. "You don't have any undercover citizens? I thought for certain Father would have had some."

The Orc shook his head. "He believed that his people feared him enough to avoid such an uprising."

At first I felt like laughing, then that realization hit deeper, dug into my brain. Now the Dragon Talon wanted to kill me.

Ûlfin turned his gaze to me. "You knew of these assassins, do you know how they recruit?"

"Rumors." I looked away, my hands clenching into fists. "Rumors that they take from soldiers that have retired or who have been forced to cycle out from injury. Nothing on how to actually find them." I spun and punched the wall, leaving a hole.

I flexed my hand, confused that the punch only stung before remembering the effects of Vycin. I would feel the hit once the medication wore off.

"They don't care the morals of their target. Just that I'm a Bubbles."
The three men looked at each other in a worried glance.
"Time will change their minds." Kutz said softly.
"But till then...." I didn't have to finish the sentence.
Ûlfin nodded, his expression grave. "I have some trusted soldiers I can send in undercover. If they're found out..." His face winced. "I hate this, spying on citizens."
"I do too." I leaned against the wall for support. "Nothing about any of this is right."
"But it has to be done, to ensure your safety." Aelyr added. "Once the Dragon Talons' are found out and exterminated then you'll be safe."
"Until then, you'll just have to stay pent up." Kutz shrugged, almost knocking a pictureframe off the wall doing so.
I watched them. Kutz trying to fix the frame he hit and somehow making it worse. Aelyr clenching his jaw, trying not to chew out his klutzy partner. Ûlfin taking a deep breath while shaking his head, shifting his weight in preparation of leaving.
"Ûlfin," I spoke softly, "lift the curfew."
His gaze darkened. "Are you certain?"
I nodded. "Yes, it makes everything a pain for doctors and those that need help. Plus removing it shows the people that I'm not a tyrant like my father before me, and his before him. It is another step in not getting me killed."
Ûlfin growled, but otherwise did not disagree. "I will pass down word, though it means your guards will have extra shifts."
We locked eyes, I would not back down. "If someone wanted to assassinate me, I don't think they'd listen to the curfew anyway." I kept my voice low, deadly serious. "Now they have to get past not just the guards of Hykur and the Red Pagoda, but also the people now free to go out at night."

Ûlfin looked away first, bowing his head in defeat of the point. "I see what you mean. I will begin passing down the orders and issuing notices."

"Thank you."

Ûlfin did not respond, rather he stormed off down the hall, for once upset with me.

I glanced between Aelyr and Kutz, both of them were watching me with interest, Aelyr with a hand resting on his sidearm.

"I'm not going to kill him." I snarled. "I'll let him get a head start and then I'm heading down to the greenhouse and botanical garden." I closed the office door. "Paperwork feels out of reach for me today anyway."

Aelyr relaxed. "Meditation is always good in times like these."

"Glad you agree with me." I tried to smile as I walked down the way Ûlfin had left. The smile didn't feel honest, even to me. I wasn't happy that I had to argue with Ûlfin, but the curfew needed to be lifted. Many customs were going to be changed.

The wait for the elevator wasn't horribly long, though the music was atrocious.

"I should have taken the stairs..." I grumbled, debating on using my aura to block my hearing.

"Honestly, we've tried changing the music," Kutz said. "it's like it's trapped on this one tune by some deep enchantment."

Aelyr laughed. "It's probably cursed by the Dragon of the Mountain itself!"

I laughed at that, a little more at ease. "If only myths were true. I sure could use help."

In short order, thankfully, the doors opened to the ground floor of the Pagoda.

FIFTEEN

The entry ground floor of the Red Pagoda was just as lavish as one would expect. Red padded benches lined the walls under large, custom paintings. The floor was a pale marble, foiled by pillars of a darker marble, each featuring red veins running through it like spiderwebs.

As in the Penthouse, hallways stretched from two of the walls, leading to libraries and other tourist traps, though the back wall was of glass and was strictly against the greenhouse and the Lords Private Botanical Garden.

As we exited the elevator more guards took up position around me, others fanning out within the people.

I made my way towards the glass wall, noting the bustling crowd had stopped and was staring. I glanced down, again I was wearing simple slacks and shirt, not anything near what the populous had grown accustomed to their Lord to wear.

I put on a smile, and beelined towards the greenhouse.

The Greenhouse itself was more of an indoor tropical forest. Birdsong came from tree branches and a large tortoise crossed my path. Again, crowds come to see the new Lord Bubbles, bowing as they backed out of my way. I didn't see the plants there, I had spent many years wandering this forest.

It was the Private Gardens that hooked my interest, that I desired to see. One of the guards at the gate unlocked it and pushed the wrought-iron gate open. The iron was worked into images of dragons, mirroring each other while surrounded my metal roses and thorny vines. I knew well those thorns were sharp as knives.

"Careful in there, Sir." The guard who had unlocked the way said, bowing slightly as I passed.

"Why?" I paused to ask. As far as I was aware there wasn't anything dangerous in the garden. Just that it was a safe sanctuary for the Lord of Farysha.

He looked around at the crowd. "I cannot say here, Sir."

I flung a hand out towards the open gate. "Then you could join me and the rest of the guards can wait out here, save Aelyr and Kutz."

He bowed again. "I would be honored, Sir."

I entered the Private Gardens, leaving the majority of the guards outside the gates. Once we walked past a few large hedges I ventured to ask the question again.

"Many plants in here are deadly, Sir." He said. "While many need to be ingested, others can either kill you or cause extreme pain just by brushing against them."

"I am assuming antidotes are on hand in case of any accidents."

He nodded. "Yes. Small vials are kept here, up against the greenhouse wall. It is enough to transport any injured to the nearest hospital for the rest of the treatment."

The nearest hospital, Hykur Memorial. I had never thought that the hospital I worked at was lined up for the emergencies of the Pagoda. I frowned. *If Hykur Memorial is for the emergencies, then why didn't any of my family show up after the attack?*

"Thank you, you may return to your post." I dismissed the guard, still deep in thought. I didn't notice him bow and leave, nor when I sat on the nearest bench.

"Is something wrong?" Aelyr asked.

"Yea," I started slowly. "I worked the emergency room at Hykur Memorial. Why wasn't any of my family brought in after the attack?

Surely the two assassins couldn't have killed all twenty of them on their own, plus however many guards as well."

The two of them shared a glance. After a moment Kutz walked down the path towards where we came, stopping by a hedge and staying just in sight.

Aelyr sat down by me. "It wasn't *just* the two assassins, per say." He looked away, acting like he was having issues coming up with how to put into words what happened that night. "One of them had been incognito for some time, working his way up the chain of command without us realizing it. Ûlfin has always had a soft spot for Orcs that want to help, so it was no surprise when Martin was given clearance. He waited like a lion stalking his prey. When he heard that everyone was coming together to plan your fathers ninetieth birthday, well, he couldn't pass up the opportunity."

He paused, glancing at me only briefly before casting his eyes to the ground. "I was on duty that day, just as new to the Penthouse as he was. When he opened fire, Harry reacted alongside the rest of your brothers." He shook his head. "Harry wasn't the only one who had gotten in the way, some had entered the crossfire from the guards, trying to take down the attackers."

I watched him as he spoke. He spoke through gritted teeth. "It's hard to say exactly what happened, it's oddly clear and cloudy in my head at the same time, but Harry started chasing them down, out of the Penthouse. I was one of the first to search for signs of life, to try to tourniquet limbs, apply pressure to torso or head wounds."

He shook his head, eyes closed. "Not one still had a heartbeat. Half the team went after Harry, shouting for him to return to the Penthouse. To return to safety. He refused."

"And he paid for his actions with his life." I muttered, looking down as well. After a moment I looked back to Aelyr. "I assume that, because it happened in the Penthouse itself, that almost none of the guard were allowed leave to help process?"

He scoffed. "Of course not. Ûlfin is working himself harder than ever, he feels like he's to blame I'm certain. He is the one who gave Martin the clearance. Once he had the clearance he was able to outfit his girlfriend to match, and guards changed enough that no one second guessed the new face."

I leaned forward, elbows on my knees. "No one gets a break anymore these days."

"That would be the truth of the matter." He agreed.

"Kutz isn't taking it easy either, I'm guessing?"

Aelyr shook his head. "No, he's not. He's using his puns and humor as a coping mechanism, much better than how others are handling it. We've already lost four of our numbers to their own actions."

"When we leave I'd like you to get a message to Ûlfin." I felt sick. Aelyr look up at me, though I still kept my own eyes downcast. "Tell him that anyone who looks, asks, or otherwise appears to need time to go home and cool off, to come to terms with what happened, to let them. If I'm not leaving the Pagoda then there's no need for a large amount of guards. I'd rather have everyone get any treatment needed than to take their own lives out of guilt." Finally I looked at him. "Ûlfin included."

The half-Elf nodded. "I will pass to him your words."

I stood, stretching. "Thank you for telling me the truth." Kutz saw me rise and returned to my side.

Finally I looked around at the garden. There were no labels, I assume that it was something Father shared with Harry, the names and effects of each plant, so there was never a need for labels from generation to generation.

A secret trap for intruders to perish while attempting to break into the back end of the Pagoda.

Aelyr and Kutz had noticed as well. "Be careful here, you two." I specifically looked at Kutz.

He smiled warmly at me, though for the first time I noted his smile was empty, his eyes appeared almost glazed over in thought. "I got it, I got it, watch myself so I don't kill myself on accident."

Aelyr flexed his jaw and silently nodded.

I glanced down, now aware of yet another issue, and one of the more important ones as well. "Kutz, seriously, there's too much going on, the world may be a terrible place, but every smile helps more than any of us realize."

His smile faded slightly, be he nodded that he understood. None of us had the time we needed to truly come to terms with what happened, and these two were there that day, as was Ûlfin. I couldn't begin to fathom how they felt, what they saw.

The red veins of he Pagoda marble took on a new meaning to me, to us. I wanted to make sure those who took care of me, kept me safe, kept me fed, kept me on track, were taken care of in turn.

"Soooo..." Kutz broke the silence. "Are we just going to stand here or what?"

"It's probably safer for you if we do." Aelyr joked. We both stared at the man. Aelyr never made jokes.

The smile on Kutz's face grew a touch more genuine, as did the soft smirk on Aelyr's.

"Then let's see what this apparently very deadly garden has to offer." I started walking forward, thinking. "Maybe we should have kept that other guy on hand as a guide."

"That other guy?" Kutz chuckled.

I shrugged. "Only reason I remembered your names is cause you two and Fitz and Hans don't seem to leave me alone. Heck I can never remember the night guards names cause I'm sleeping while they're probably playing board games outside my bedroom door."

"Rock, Paper, Scissors." Kutz corrected. "But they're Josh and Grüdar."

Spinning I rose my finger in the air. "Aha! And I'll forget that they totally goof off at night AND their names before I go to bed and they take over for Hans and Fitz."

Kutz rubbed the back of his head. "At least you're not calling us all Steve like Harry did."

I turned back to the front and laughed. "Harry had the brains of a goldfish."

I swear I heard them both mumble "Not wrong" under their breaths.

The Private Garden was unique in a way that is difficult to describe. There were some plants that were kept behind intricate fencing, others that climbed on matching trellises, and yet more that grew in raised beds, cascading over the sides.

Trident leaves that I recognized as belonging to Nightshade, the most common of these deadly plants in Farysha, grew everywhere. More than once have I had a patient come in after eating the berries.

While the garden might seem like a cacophony of colors spread from leaves to berries to flowers, there was an unnatural type of cohesion to the whole scene. It kept you moving from one plant to another, just enough time between each to focus on it, see the details, before the colors of the next caught your attention.

So it was that we went around the garden twice before noon came, and we paused on a bench near some rather gorgeous purple flowers boasting bright red centers.

"Remind me to make sure I get a tour guide next time, I would really like to know what's all in here." I noted, watching the flower.

"Intend to use some of them against your enemies?" Aelyr asked.

I shook my head. "No, more for my own safety. And that of Kutz, of course."

Kutz laughed at that. "Hey, I've been doing rather well today." He looked up at the sky. "Though if we keep our feet planted here then I'm sure Hans and Fitz will get worried."

Aelyr groaned at the pun. "He is right, sadly. This place is definitely of interest to me as well."

I smiled, smelling the flower before me. It smelled like lilies and lilac, two of my mothers favorites. "Then let's be off." I said, standing straight.

I wobbled, suddenly dizzy.

Aelyr was first at my side. "Lord? Is your injuries bothering you again?" I shook my head. "No... the Vycin is still working.." I tried to stand again, but couldn't. "Go get the guard or whoever tends to this garden. I need to kn-"

Aelyr caught my full weight as my legs went numb and vision blurred. It was getting hard to focus. I thought I saw Kutz take off towards the entrance.

I was thankful that Aelyr had me, as blackness overtook my sight I was certain that those bricks that made up the paths would be rather painful to land on.

As unconsciousness came to me, I could swear I saw Aelyr wobble slightly as well.

SIXTEEN

I dreamed of voices, familiar yet long gone. Of bright lights and prodding pinches.

But for the most part, the only think I remembered after the bricks and someone catching me, was cold darkness.

I came to in a bright room, a familiar room with a white ceiling, but I couldn't remember why it was familiar. *Why do I remember this place? Where am I?*

I closed my eyes, and again the darkness consumed me.

When I next woke I chose not to open my eyes. I felt calmer, lighter than I had. Breathing was easier, but my head still pounded, as did my side. Something annoying was pinching at the back of my wrists.

I wasn't alone.

"How much did he take in?" A womans voice asked. "He should be awake by now."

"We all stood by the flowers for a while, though he was closest." An elegant mans voice responded. "Kutz and myself did start feeling effects, we even passed out or some time, though the antidote seems to have done its' job for us."

She sighed, though I wasn't sure what emotion was tied to it. "Why did he even go in there?" She asked softly, almost to herself it seemed.

"I'm not fully certain. I assumed he would want to visit as it is his private gardens now, at least to see what is inside, so he'd know if something were to occur. Or, maybe, he wanted to be more alone than is allowed in the Penthouse, it does get very busy and after all that's happened..."

"After all that's happened some alone time is always a blessing." She finished his sentence.

Now I remembered her name. Hope. Pieces were coming together. I had to be in one of the triage rooms. But that couldn't be right.....

I dared a deeper breath as I slowly opened my eyes, wincing at the bright lights. I wasn't on any breathing tubes, but I had been on one recently. An oxygen mask was still on my face in lieu of tubes up my nose which ached.

The room went abnormally silent. The light was too bright, I closed my eyes again.

"That's a good sign." Hope said in a sigh of relief.

I tried talking, to say "of course it is," but it didn't come out nearly as I had wanted.

"It's ok Stan, we got you. Just rest." Hope said, patting my hand over the IV needle.

I half opened an eye at her, happy that she didn't seem upset with me, but at the same time angry that she hadn't said a word over the past four days.

"Don't give me that look." She snorted out of habit before allowing a soft smile to take over her features. I noted her hair was tied up in a bow with Faryshan colors today instead of her normal deep violet.

I closed my eye again and took another deep breath, this time adding the word "bright" rather successfully.

"On it." I felt her hand leave mine, and half the lights in the room went dark.

Slowly I opened my eyes fully.

Though the world was still blurry I recognized the room, Hope, and Aelyr. I tried to move to find the remote to sit the bed up, but my thoughts were moving like slugs and my hand wouldn't move.

I felt my brows furrow in frustration.

"Stop trying to move." Hope appeared at my side again. "And no I'm not letting you sit up until Kronda gets a good look at you again."

Well, speaking was near impossible right now, so I rolled my eyes.

"Of course he's the one in charge of you!" Hope put her hands on her hips. "Did you really expect to treat yourself while you've been unconscious for two days?"

My head snapped to her surprisingly fast. I felt dizzy again, closing my eyes to stop the world from spinning. I had tp be extra careful for some time to avoid a longer coma.

"You know how bad that is," She whispered, "so you should know well the procedures that have to be done." I felt her light lips leave a kiss on my forehead. I must have worried her deeply for such a show, especially in front of another. "I'll go fetch Kronda, I'll tell him to be nice."

I tried to nod, it came slow, like I was moving though caramel.

I felt Aelyr come sit by my side. His aura was warm, with a few touches of refreshing cool. It reminded me of an early summer breeze, before the wind has had time to warm up all the way.

"Apparently there are a few flowers in the garden that can incapacitate people with their pollen." He started, knowing I'd be curious as to what happened. "Of course they were bred to be the best smelling ones, so they lure in their victims." He paused.

I opened my eyes again to watch him. His body was half turned from me, his face completely in shame. This time I put more focus, more will, into moving my hand. I placed it on his arm, rather than the shoulder like I was hoping for, and managed a comforting squeeze.

He turned to look at me, he looked like he was beat up by something.

"The pollen got to Kutz and myself as well." He continued, looking back at the floor as he spoke. "We're on leave, according to Ûlfin, to heal up. But we couldn't just leave you here, so we're taking turns."

He grew quiet, letting the silence stretch on. Kronda would take his time, especially if he was already attending to another patient.

"I passed out as soon as we got you in the ambulance." Aelyr continued. "Kutz once we got you here. We were out for about ten hours, each. He woke up first."

I wanted to tell him to go home, to rest. But I knew he wouldn't listen. So we sat there, Aelyr looking at the floor, for some reason shamed, with my hand on his arm.

I squeezed again, feeling worse that I couldn't do anything to ease the suffering of a man who had taken my safety on such a personal level. I felt that he blamed himself.

I should have kept someone who knew the plants on hand, this whole debacle was mine to take the blame. Not only did I endanger myself, I put my own men at risk.

Again. First the funeral, again with the garden.

My first week as Lord of Farysha was not going well.

We both looked over as the door opened and an olive-toned Dwarf with blonde hair and beard came in. "Ah Stan, what did ya go and do this time?" He asked, shaking his head.

I rolled my eyes and shook my head as Aelyr answered. "Poison flower, one of the custom bred ones of the garden."

"And thankfully yer gardenkeeper ensured we 'ave plenty 'o antidote in case this happened." He said, pulling a stool over to the side of the bed, making the half-Elf move.

Aelyr didn't complain, but watched the Dwarf like both our lives depended on it.

"Aelyr...." I tried saying, again using the same focus and will I normally would spend on my magic just to speak, "I trust him."

His golden rimed lilac eyes flicked to me before returning to the Dwarf. Right now, he didn't trust anyone. He was about to be in for a surprise with Doctor Goldenbeard.

It was me, however, that was in for a surprise. Normally Kronda was rather rough with me in passing, not like a bully but more like an older brother trying to be funny. Today he was abnormally gentle checking my vitals.

I was a good patient and did exactly as I was told to the letter. It only took a few minutes and a couple blood samples to test for how much toxin still remained in my system.

Aelyr was trying to stop him from leaving the room with my blood, knowing what dangers that could entail.

Kronda snarled at him. "Look, boy, I know full well the aura attachment laws in regards to blood and magic. I also 'ave known Stan for ten years, since he came to work 'ere, so I reckon I know 'im better than ya. I also know that our lab is filled to the brim with little folk that don't take kindly to intrusions. It'll be burned once the testing is done."

The half-Elf stumbled back to his seat. I chuckled a bit. He looked at me with a not very serious glare. "You could have said something."

I raised an eyebrow and weakly pointed towards my face. "Words hard." I managed to spurt out.

Kronda laughed heartily. "And cause 'o that ya should keep yer yap shut till I say so, Stan."

I tried giving him a look, noting that he wasn't using any titles, Doctor nor Lord.

He smiled at that, "Yer my patient, and 'ave been a friend for a decade. I think we're past petty words."

That made me smile and relax. Neither Hope nor Kronda seemed to be angry at me for leaving, for the lies. For the atrocities of my family.

But why was I still in triage, not in the ICU? Kronda had disappeared before I got a chance to ask.

Ûlfin entered the room shortly after Kronda left. He paused, looking at Aelyr. "I thought I gave you leave." He said more than asked.

Aelyr shrugged. "Just getting a follow up exam."

The Orc towered over me, obviously displeased. "I turn my back on you for less than a day and you try to kill yourself?" He asked through gritted teeth.

I looked away, shame and embarrassment filling me. I hadn't meant to, but somewhere deep down....

I pushed the thought aside before it could emerge from the emotional surge. People were depending on me to be better than my predecessors, I couldn't do that if I were dead.

Aelyr appeared next to Ûlfin, placating. "None of us knew that area was infested with deadly pollen. If I had I would have made sure proper safety equipment was used."

I looked at the men nodding and pointing at Aelyr.

Ûlfin didn't seem quite content. "Not speaking now?"

I looked at the half-Elf for help. He obliged. "Doctor Goldenbeard says that the way the pollen works is by knocking out the amount of oxygen you get from your lungs. After that your lungs and body go into overdrive trying to get any oxygen to your brain. He doesn't want the Lord straining himself nor his lungs needlessly." His gaze flicked to me for a moment before returning to the tall Orc. "Besides, he's been having trouble speaking after being unconscious the past two days."

"You seem to be doing fine."

"My mother's of Elven blood." Aelyr growled. Elves had an unnaturally fast recovery rate, we rarely saw them in the hospital as patients. "I was discharged last night, Kutz this morning."

I thought I saw Ûlfins' shoulders relax some. He had been worried about more than just me.

I tried sitting up, I wanted to know why I hadn't been moved to the ICU like procedures called for. Both the men looked down at me.

"Stay still." They said at once.

I huffed and gave up on trying. I didn't have much in me, I'd probably have fallen over had I succeeded at sitting up anyway. I noted the room was slowly getting dimmer, I guessed that I had been already overexerting myself.

All the same, I needed to know. Again I gathered my will and focus to speak. "Why still here?" I managed to ask. "Why no ICU?"

Just those words left me with more exhaustion than I had felt all week. I closed my eyes, but remained awake. I just didn't have the energy to keep them open anymore. I knew unconsciousness was not far away. Ûlfin answered me. "Your doctor, your friends here. They want to make sure you get well, not anyone else. They're refusing to let you out of this room, and are severely limiting who is allowed in."

Despite how tired I was, I felt a smile come to my face.

SEVENTEEN

After two days of recovery I was finally able to sit up and walk around for a few minutes. Kronda still didn't want me to talk, but I had tested my ability and found speech was healing just as well as the rest of me. Eventually I was put up in a private room near the ICU but not exactly within, "just in case" I was told by Kronda. I pulled some strings so they could remain my attending physician and nurses.

I had gotten a chance to speak more to Hope and Sera, thankfully. They explained that the silence was in part due to them having no idea what to even say to me, I had just lost everything I had for a life I didn't want. Another part was how busy they were. A riot had broken out the day after I had left, and of course no one had told me.

Thankfully everything had calmed down, and I had just not checked my phone nor email at all after the funeral. Hope had showed me that they had tried calling and sent messages asking how I was holding up.

The truth is, at the time I really wasn't holding up at all. Not until my talk with Aleyna.

I had been thinking of her more often as of late. More than likely because she had been the first to sit down and want to listen, want to talk, and understood. She had lost a brother, she was now the Crown Princess.

I dreamed of her too, and of Hope and Sera, during my long periods of sleep. I was certain Kronda was sneaking something to me to make me rest longer. I would if I were in his place, knowing my patient wanted nothing more than to get up and get work done.

One morning, or rather afternoon, I awoke to King Jean in my room, staring out the window, his crown sitting upon the sill. He wasn't dressed in the fineries of silks I had grown accustomed to him wearing, rather he wore a simple suit of gray, untucked with his hands resting in his pockets.

I glanced around, seeing none of the faces I usually woke up to, specifically Aelyr and Kutz who rarely left my side while they waited for Ûlfin to let them back on duty. I didn't mind my hospital stay, even though I was well enough to return to the Pagoda, because I knew it gave them something to do.

Once I returned they'd have to wait until they were cleared by Ûlfin, and Gods be damned I liked those two around too much to go even a day without their antics.

It wasn't until I stood up to join him at the window that Jean noticed I was awake.

"I hope zat you do not mind ze intrusion." He asked, still looking out the window.

"Not at all, Your Majesty." I responded, trying to find what he was so focused on. I could see nothing but buildings and the occasional park.

He scoffed lightly. "Please, just Jean right now. After all, I am intruding upon your rest."

My turn to laugh, albeit significantly more than Jean did. "Kronda is a friend, he knows that the moment he clears me to leave I will go straight back to work." I glanced back at the chair where one of my guards usually was glued to. "Besides, two of my personal guard are still on leave and refuse to be far from me. It wouldn't be fair to go back without them."

Finally, he glanced aside at me, the golden rims of his irises shimmering with the light. "And should zey fall sick and cannot work?"

"Then perhaps I should visit them, as they so took care of me. Especially with Kutz I would make jokes. Aelyr would do best with a good book." I returned my attention to him. "Of course Ûlfin would have back-ups waiting to step in until they are healed, and probably does now for my return."

"Could you not check yourself out?"

I smiled, thinking of Krondas' expression if I did. "I could. I mean, no one would stop me. But it would hurt the friends I have here. So, I'll play along for now."

My expression sobered and I looked down. "It has given me ample time to think in solitude, to relax, and to better accept all that has happened over the past week." My eyes returned to Jean. "I hope your travels have served you in a similar fashion."

His expression grew blank, though only for an instant before he returned his gaze to the city view. "It has. I have had much to think about, to consider." He blinked a few times before looking around and sitting on the edge of the bed, leaning forward like a man who has to make tough choices far too often.

He aged in that instance. Rather than the young-looking king of Elven blood his human side was showing. Wrinkles marred his forehead, crows feet touched his eyes, and his shoulders sagged.

"Aleyna is ze last child I have. With my passing she will continue on with ze Crown. But she was not raised to lead, Eryk was."

I sat beside him. "Neither was I." I whispered. "I was just along for the ride, living my own life as best I could. She has time to learn, to be a good queen."

Though he nodded his expression was still distant. "She was trained to be a wife, Stan. As is ze way with younger women of courtly lines. Yes, she will still be trained now to take over as Queen of Bisney, it was never her original intentions."

I watched him, somewhat confused as to where he was going.

"I decided to ask of you more zan I am entitled to, as King of Bisney or as just Jean." His eye met mine.

I leaned back in sudden realization. Indeed, he was stepping out of line, but at the same time, he wasn't. To most this would seem a typical political transaction.

"A true merger of Bisney and Farysha." He continued, "If at least for but a single generation. Our complete forces would be at your disposal."

The Dragon Riders of the Southern Black Mountains. With them Paryda would fall with haste. He could not offer them to the Lord of Farysha, but he *could* to a future son in law and heir in order to protect the life of his own daughter.

"Is the Prin-" I started, cutting myself off midword, "is Aleyna in agreement with this?"

"She is." Came Jeans' curt reply.

I stood, staring out the window but not at anything in specific. "How long is your visit?"

Though he watched me he did not rise. "We would stay a few more days, no more zan four."

"Then I will give you my answer in three days time, if it pleases you." I turned to look at him. "This is bigger than just who I wed, this," I stumbled for words, waving my hands at everything, "involves everyone."

"I understand." He stood to leave. "I shall await you in ze Penthouse."

Jean retrieved his crown, bowed slightly deeper than he should have, and left before I had time to react.

Though I knew such a marriage would be best for Farysha, Bisney did have the best economy and air force on the continent of Asura, I thought of Hope and Sera, of the feelings I had for them. I feared how heartbroken they would be, how miserable Aleyna might be.

I continued to stare out the window, at nothing but the sky and the monotonous gray of the city, until I could no longer stand and night was beginning to fall.

EIGHTEEN

Kronda discharged me that night, and Ûlfin cleared Aelyr and Kutz to return to work.

I was sitting at my desk, feeling more awake than I had while in the hospital. Of course that only confirmed my theory that Kronda was giving me sleeping medication every time he came in to check on me and bring me food.

A report from Ahun sat on my desk, requesting additional medical support on the front lines. I had just sent emails off to Hykur Memorial and others across the country requesting that they send all they can to help, and decided that I would join them.

But still I sat, staring at nothing, debating the request of Jean. He trusted me enough to watch over his sole heir, his only remaining child. I was honored, yes, but felt foolish at the same time.

I looked up when a runner knocked on the door. Hans and Fitz were standing guard, glaring at the poor woman and making her feel uncomfortable.

"Go ahead and speak." I said, gently.

She nodded, but hesitated before speaking. "The Head of Guard would like to see you in his office."

I rose an eyebrow at her. Ûlfin never asked for me to come to him, normally it was the other way around. I rose and had her lead the way to the Orcs' office.

Ûlfin resided on the other side of the Penthouse, his office was sparsely furnished, his achievements and rankings on the wall in frames, a flag of Farysha on one side behind him, mirrored by a flag showing the emblem of the Farysha Guard.

To either side of the door, both inside and outside, stood two guards. Just inside the door, on the floor, was a thick, yellow line. I stopped behind it, gaining side glances from the two inside the room. I thought I saw one of them smirk at the other.

Ûlfin looked up and smiled. "Lord, you don't need to stop there." He motioned me to stand besides him.

I did so. "What's this about?" I asked. "I need to speak to you then Brock in private about a matter as well."

I looked at me, I thought I saw a twitch in an eye. He returned his gaze to the two men at the door, he nodded to one of them.

He was being oddly formal, I was worried it was because of the argument we had. I hoped it did not diminish our friendship to that of mearly workplace politeness.

The man left and returned within the minute. Three other men followed, each more decorated than the ones standing at the door, each as much as Ûlfin I noted. They had stopped hard at the line and did not cross.

"Lord Bubbles, may I introduce my Chief Warrant Officers: Officer Kyblar, Head of Pagoda Detail, Officer Haylo, Head of the City Guards, and Officer Jinay, Head of the Border. They are second in command to me."

I nodded at the three in turn at greeting. Each was an Elf, though Officer Jinay may have only been half. "It is an honor to finally meet you three."

They each returned a similar phrase of greeting.

"They normally reside elsewhere, save for Officer Kyblar, and relay messages to me to coordinate their efforts. However, as I have chosen to take a week of leave, they will be standing in my place, each taking shifts throughout the day."

"I will be sad that you are gone," I looked at Ûlfin who was at my eye level seated, "though I am glad you are taking time for yourself. You do much here, and I am ever grateful for all you accomplish."

"You flatter me, Sir." He smiled, half turning to me, but still keeping an eye at the men in the room.

I turned to the other men in the room. "Before I dismiss each of you, I should probably inform you three as well. I intend to leave soon, to join other doctors to assist those who are injured. I would like a small retinue of guards and soldiers, so that I may continue to be informed of occurrences that it is on me to decide, and so that I am protected until such a time as an heir is apparent."

The three broke protocol and shared looks at each other, a move Ûlfin did not care to correct as he himself was staring at me, slack jawed. The other two guards remained stonefaced.

"Stan," Ûlfin objected, "it is not safe enough out there for you."

I shrugged. "I won' be on the front lines proper, but I am used to working in emergency situations. I know it's different than battle, but it's how I can help, and I won't sit by and do nothing." I looked back at the other three. "As I intend to leave before Ûlfin returns, any guest I may permit to remain here I want you to ensure is protected as if they were me, understood?"

"Understood, Sir!" They each shouted, including the two by the door.

"Then you are all dismissed." I said, "I need to speak to Ûlfin in private." I waited till all five left, closing the door behind them, before walking around to the other side of the desk, noting the lack of chairs.

"Stan, what's wrong?" His already worn face looked like he couldn't bear much more.

"I need your opinion on an offer by King Jean."

He motioned for me to continue. I paced the room as I talked. "He has asked if I would take his daughter as my wife. We would unite Bisney and Farysha, at least for our generation if not for the rest of time should we have only one child."

He leaned back in his chair, shock taking over where weariness had taken hold.

"In this offer is the complete use of the Dragon Riders." I stopped, looking Ûlfin in the eyes. "That alone could win us the war."

He ran his fingers over his head. "Ahun would know more about the Parydan army, though I do believe they hold no type of air force." He rested his hands on the desk, meeting my eyes. "The Riders would be a force to be reckoned with, and their Navy, alongside our own, would stop any leaders from leaving from their shores."

"But, this means, especially if we fully merge the countries, that laws must be changed in the merger."

Ûlfin sat in thought, mulling ideas over in his head. "We can make it work. I am certain that the guards would enjoy having less laws and mandates that are insanely strict, and that the populous would enjoy a smaller tax rate."

"So you believe the merger would be a good idea?"

"For Farysha, yes." He stood up and came to me. "For you, I am not sure."

I gave him a quizzical look.

He sighed and continued. "If your heart isn't in it, then the marriage won't work."

"I do care for her, but I only just met her."

"My suggestion, then, is that you accept with an addendum. Give it a few months of living together, here in the Penthouse, before the wedding, to ensure that the marriage will last."

"If it doesn't then I look like I used the Kings' good graces and may have gained an enemy." I noted.

He shrugged, at a loss for words. "I have made my suggestion."

"It is probably the course of action I will take." I gestured that I wanted him to take his seat back. "One more thing, Ûlfin. Should anything happen to me, either here or on the field, I have written up documents to name you as my heir until such time a child of my bloodline is born and reaches eighteen years of age."

He looked down at the desk, sadness entering his features which looked to have gotten a shade more pale. "What of Brock?"

"We are in a time of war, plus I am more confident in you as I have known you longer. You were always more of a father to me than my own. I am certain Brock will understand." I looked away. "I know I hope you do."

"Stan," he whispered, "I do, and I am honored at your choice, though I hope that day never comes."

"As do I." I took a deep breath and looked around the room again. "I shall take my leave and allow you to prepare for your vacation."

"Thank you, Stan." Ûlfin said, warmly. "Your words mean more to me than you know."

I smiled at him over my shoulder. "You mean more to me than you know, you always have."

With that I left the room, sending a runner to Brock to have him meet me in my office.

Brock gave the same answer as Ûlfin had, to agree but request to wait for the wedding until a few months had passed. There was but one more person I needed to talk to about the decision: Princess Aleyna.

She came to my office completely unsummoned before I chose to close up and search for her.

"Lord Bubbles," she started, "zere was something I desired to speak to you about."

I stood and beckoned her to sit, joining her in the other chair instead of my normal seat. "I wanted to talk to you as well."

She nodded and daintily took the chair, sitting with practiced poise. "I know of what my father has asked of you."

Straight to the point then. I nodded, taking a calming breath. "That is what I wished to discuss with you as well. I cannot accept if you are not willing."

She smiled. "I am. I know we barely know each other, but I am not opposed to such a union."

"Oh?"

"It's, difficult to explain." She scratched the back of her head. "My family has always had an inkling of magic use, each of us in our own ways. Father can sense power and intellect, I can sense personality."

"And you believe ours compatible?"

"Yes. I do."

I smiled. "This will take some getting used to." I said, mostly to myself.

"I do not understand."

"My father never let me find a wife, nor date much to be honest." I leaned on my knees. "I was never allowed to have children, heirs that could threaten the rule of the first borns. I always fancied the idea of settling down, but I knew if I did, he would quickly kill any I wed."

"Zat sounds terrible." Aleyna placed her hands on mine.

I lifted one of mine and placed it on hers, they were small and warm. A gentle comfort.

"For a while I fancied I would be with Hope or Sera." I whispered.

"Ze nurses?" She watched me. "Zey were nice and friendly."

"I've known them for years, well, Hope for years, Sera was still rather new at the hospital." I looked back up to her. "I couldn't let my father hurt them, so I didn't let them fancy me."

"He cannot hurt anyone anymore." She said, moving a hand to my cheek. "Let us take our time, and see what happens. I think we may yet be good, though I do not wish to hurt your heart."

I smiled. "My heart has been hurt long ago. I do not think I can be with them, emergency life is hard, and they would not enjoy the dangers we are accustomed to."

She nodded her agreement.

"There is one other thing. I have chosen to go out and aid in the war effort as more doctors are needed. Ûlfin is taking leave for a week, so I have ordered that if you choose to remain after your father leaves that you are to be treated with the utmost respect."

"I hope zat zere are not any issues."

I sighed and leaned back. "I don't think that you'll have any issues once we announce our engagement." I laughed suddenly. "I'll have to find a good ring for you, I don't have one on hand."

She blushed but smiled.

Yes, I think I can get used to this.

NINETEEN

King Jean was scheduled to leave that day, he did not join me for breakfast. I wasn't certain if Aleyna gave him my answer or not, but he had been staying in his room upstairs for the most part.

I did not bother him.

When he wanted to talk to me he would send someone or seek me out himself.

So it was that I was in the middle of the preparations and paperwork to leave Brock in charge of the Penthouse and Pagoda alongside the three Chief Warrant Officers, while I was away in Paryda when he walked in the door, ignoring Hans and Fitz.

I stood as he walked to my desk, taking a seat in one of the two chairs.

"My daughter has informed me zat you are to leave."

I nodded. "Yes. I will be going with other doctors and nurses to the battles to assist where I may."

"I am pleased zat you have accepted my offer."

"You understand that we both wish to hold off a wedding for at least a few months, in case we are utterly incompatible." I remained standing behind my desk.

"I am in agreement." He said curtly. I noted a significant personality difference between when he was in his role as King versus when he can relax and be himself.

"If Her Highness wishes to remain or return to the Penthouse while I am gone I have already issued orders that my fiance is to be treated as such, and with as much respect as I would be treated." I noted a small smile touch his lips. "She will be safe, and the only area that will be off limits is the Private Gardens after my incident."

"I believe zat you have made zem "off limits" to yourself as well, at least for some time." The King noted.

I chuckled. "Yea, I am not ready to return to that place until labels of what the plant is, the effects, and the antidote name are all properly installed." I glanced downwards for a moment before returning my gaze to the man before me. "Is this acceptable to Your Majesty?"

"It is, especially as my daughter has found it acceptable well before I had a chance to discuss zis with her." I heard a tinge of irritation that Aleyna had decided something on her own, without him, but also a soft sense of pride that she was learning more of her new role.

He stood, extending his arm. We clasped at the elbows, a sign of friendliness and respect rather than the traditional handshake.

"It was an honor to meet you, Lord Stan, and is an honor to know zat you will be a part of my family."

I smiled, a touch of sadness I knew had grown in my features. "The honor is mine, Your Majesty, becoming a part of a family greater than my own, I cannot express my gratitude."

He smiled as well. "It is, as one would say, poetic." We released each other and straightened. "I have lost a son and will be gaining one, and you have lost a father, and will be gaining one."

My eyes dropped to my desk, that which had been my fathers, my grandfathers, all the way to when Farysha became a country. Silence hung in the air between us. It was a busy week, and I knew we both wished such a meeting were under better circumstances.

"It is time." He turned to leave, but paused. "Aleyna has requested to remain here, I will send items she requests upon my arrival to ze Castle of Dawn." He shifted to face me once more. "I will also send orders ahead of me to ze Riders to report to High General Ahun and yourself. Zey will be at your disposal, do not risk ze lives of my men needlessly."

"I will not, Your Majesty." I squared my shoulders and set my jaw. I was hoping for this response but doubted I would receive the reinforcements with the delayed wedding and me running off to the battles. "And all of Farysha thanks you, we know that the Riders can mean the difference between our failure and success."

He nodded. "May ze Gods bless ze air under your wings."

"And may the fires of the mountain keep you warm."

He smiled, bowed deeply at the waist, somehow his crown did not fall off, and departed. I watched the empty doorway for some time, feeling oddly empty.

I knew Aleyna would keep a small retinue of guards and personal assistants here with her, but most of the people they brought with would leave with the King. Everyone that had been cycled out to make room for the extra attendants would be returning tomorrow, so the usual bustle of the Pagoda would remain.

But I would be gone too.

I was set to leave tomorrow, Ahun had already gotten me armor, uniform, and all the rest of the gear I would need to stand in as an Army Medic. In place of the rankings a single, flying dragon stood on a large red cross. Everything was stored in my closet, borderline on display on a table and hanging besides it, so as not to wrinkle or destroy any aspect. Dealing with the aftermath of riots was one thing, full on combat I knew will be something else.

I wasn't certain I was ready for it.

So I did the biggest thing I knew to do, and continued on paperwork. I didn't keep track of the time, just worked on reviewed laws, signing them out of being active where needed.

Eventually Brock came into the room, yawning. "What are ya still doing here?" He asked.

"Work."

"Ya gotta go in the morning, or did ya change your plans?"

I stopped and just stared at the page I was on, something about tax rates, not really moving nor wanting to.

"Stan? Ya okay?" Brock asked.

I took a deep breath and rubbed my eyes. "Sorry Brock, I'm just nervous I guess."

"You'll be fine." He said, hopping up on a chair to see over the desk. "Yer a medic, not a soldier, so ya won't be on the front lines."

"I will be, at one point. I won't be able to avoid it."

"Clan match to gain control of Paryda?" Of course he knew the Parydan laws.

"Yea, it's the only way to end this, one way or another."

Brock looked away, concern on his face. "If yer champion looses...."

"That's why I'm nervous." I glanced out the door, feeling the weight of rule on my shoulders. "It's a gamble, and Farysha is at risk if we fail."

Brock scoffed. "Farysha will live under your heir. You will have to be at the fight. Your life is at risk if you fail."

The words hung in the air like deadly threads of wire. Neither of us moved in fear of getting cut. Neither said another word in fear of getting caught by emotions.

This plan depended on that one moment.

Brock hopped down from the chair with a rather impressive sounding thump. "Get some sleep, lad. Ya don't know when yer next chance to sleep will be after tonight."

I nodded, a lump in my throat preventing me from speaking. I have only been a Lord for a week, yet by next I could be resting upon my own funeral pyre, or more likely left in some muddy hole in the ground without ceremony.

Awkwardly I managed to sort the papers into done and to do piles, and slowly closed the door to the office, leaning against it slightly. Hans and Fitz had retired, Josh and Grüdar had taken over.

They tailed me down the hall to my own room, and remained outside when I entered and closed the door. I ran my fingers over the polished gleam of the Collar of Estate, proudly displayed. My hand stopped on the pendant, on the Sleeping Dragon of Farysha.

There was a legends, a childrens tale, that I had not thought of for a long time. It spoke of a dragon that once called this land his home. Once my ancestors arrived here the dragon chose to live in peace with them, sleeping deep in the volcano. When the people came under attack and were under threat of total annihilation the dragon emerged with a flow of lava and destructive clouds, destroying the threat in one pass before returning to his slumber.

I wondered if it were more than just a tall tale mothers told their children when they were scared.

I was scared now.

Silently, as I crawled into bed, my cat jumping up to purr on my chest, I prayed. I prayed to the Gods to give me strength, to give Ahun strength and speed. And I prayed to the dragon for courage, and for him to protect my people if we failed.

Despite my fears, no dreams came to me that night.

TWENTY

I stared at myself in the mirror. I was in uniform.

I felt like an imposter.

Ahun had requested that I join his platoon with haste, and wear the full armored get up.

The helmet felt awkward and top heavy, the gorget around my neck pinched in places and the collar on my under shirt would not stay up long enough to help the cut-resistant fabric from rubbing against my skin. The body armor was bulky, and had tools, extra magazines, and other small items of necessity. Even more, including my sword, pistol, and an emergency trauma kit hung from my belt. More tools and equipment were in my pockets down my leg, and a spare knife was tucked inside my boot.

By my feet were two bags. The larger of which had spare clothes and a few backup emergency trauma kits. The other bag held a full medical range of items, and would serve as my primary resource in the field.

I looked awkward, like everything was a size or two too big.

I barely moved my head when there was a knock at my open door. Aelyr popped his head in, looking around. The attendants who helped me get dressed had already left.

"Sir, transport is ready for you."

"Thank you, Aelyr." I grabbed my bags, tossing one over each shoulder. They were both heavy, but I didn't complain.

"Should we send for assistants to carry your bags?"

"No, if my soldiers need to do this than so will I."

Aelyr smiled at that and said nothing else. They had their own bags with them, as did Josh and Grüdar, and Hans and Fitz. All six were coming with and were dressed in their battle gear as I was. Their shoulders had rankings with a tongue of flame in the center, marking them as personal guards to the Lord and generally second to me.

Together, looking like a cohesive unit, we made our way down to the lobby. The elevator music was still insanely irritating and Kutz and Hans started singing random songs as loud as they could. Aelyr tried to cover his ears at the sound, but was smiling to himself.

Crowds cleared faster today than they had when I visited the garden. That day I had been in casual clothes, even for most people, today I was dressed for battle and every single soul knew it. Everyone there saw it.

The Lord of Farysha going to join his men in combat.

Something that had not been done in the memory of anyone alive.

Together we climbed into an armored transport vehicle. They had offered something more comfortable, a limousine or something alike, but I had turned them down.

I needed the men to see me down at their level. I needed them to understand that I was different. That I was willing to risk my life to save theirs.

The ride was bumpy and we were jostled around. Our driver had said that we were going straight to where Ahun was sitting, taking heavy fire as he neared Hastengrad, the capital of Paryda where Ukzahg sat upon his throne. It would take our caravan two whole days to reach the High General, and those with us that could drive the large truck were to take turns driving.

Our only stops were to be to refuel from the tankers with us and to relieve our bladders.

For the first few hours no one spoke. We sat in silence, fretting the first sounds of battle. Some of those with me knew what to expect, and their faces were as pale as ash knowing they were to potentially see combat once again.

My guards knew they would see battle, and that we might have to fight for our lives to escape.

They knew we might not return alive, if at all. Parydans were particularly nasty in regards to what they do with the bodies of enemies. We held no fancies that, should we fall, that our loved ones would see us again.

Kutz was the one who chose to break the silence. First he tried some jokes, none of them were any good though Hans laughed heartily. Eventually the two took to singing boisterously.

It wasn't but a song or two before the rest of us joined in, smiling despite our nerves, our fears.

As night fell we leaned against each other to sleep. I don't think any of us managed to rest much at all.

The second day was a repeat of the first, sitting on a bench in silence, our bags on the floor before us.

During our periodic breaks to refuel I managed to talk to those in the rest of the caravan. Kronda had come with, though Hope and Sera chose to remain at the hospital. We were glad, both the nurses were filled with joy and didn't need to come with, to lose that spark in their eyes and the warmth in their smiles.

"How's yer ribs?" He had asked me at one of the stops.

"Sore, but healing." I glanced back at the trucks. "The rough ride is not doing the healing any good."

"Just take the Vycin as needed, we can't 'ave you falling over in pain while we're 'ere."

I smiled at him as it was time to load back up. ""Don't worry so much about me, Kronda, let's worry about the men we're here to help."

He walked off murmuring something about worrying about whoever he feels like. I got back in my seat, rubbing my side that ached more than I had let on.

The stops also allowed me to look at the Parydan landscape. The Black Mountains had quickly given way to thick forests and reeking swamps.

Grüdar had warned not to enter swamps with a small pathway, claiming Ogres lived in there and were more fearful than Orcs when enraged. Thankfully Ogres were hermits and as long as they were left alone they did not care who was in charge of what.

The road we were on had been built up and was halfway a bridge most of the time, built of logs and rough stone which only caused us to bounce around even more in the trucks.

But as we rode on, Kutz and Hans sung more. We each sang our favorite songs, joining in on ones we knew. We joked that by the time we arrived we will have all lost our voices and would be considered to crazy to remain.

As night fell on the second day we came to a stop and jumped out of the truck. Coming around to the lead I saw what was blocking us; a massive black dragon with a rider in the saddle.

The Riders had arrived before us.

The figure on the back of the dragon slid down the arm of the wing and landed before us. "State your name and business."

I stepped forward. "Lord Doctor Stan Bubbles of Farysha, with retinue of guards, soldiers, doctors, and nurses along with needed supplies."

He came up and met me, taking his helmet off to reveal a handsome Elven face with eyes that I knew would be violet, but appeared black in the dark of night. "I am Captain Fíla, and this is Blackthorn. We have been expecting your arrival and will escort you to High General Ahun."

"Thank you." I bowed slightly. "Lead the way."

Everyone once again climbed in back of the trucks and we drove off, hearing the drumming of dragon wings above us.

Within a few minutes we heard more drums and soft roars.

We had arrived.

TWENTY ONE

Dragons of various colors soared in formation over the encampment. Large brick-shaped containers of water and dirt formed the walls around us, some of which had been made so that gates could be attached. Each were at least five feet in width, featuring interlocking ridges around the lengthy top sides and a smoother center so that patrols could walk upon them as mock battlements.

Tents were spaced around the interior, which I noted was a maze made up of the same containers. Somewhere, in what I assumed was the center, a flagpole rose high with the Faryshian flag, the slumbering red dragon flying lazily in the breeze.

High General Ahun stood at attention as we strode forward, besides him was every soldier that could be spared. As one they snapped their hands to their foreheads in a salute, which I promptly returned in as serious a manner as I could muster.

"High General Ahun, soldiers, please take your ease." I said, willing my aura to increase my volume. "If you have duties to attend to please see to them. I do not wish to have everything put on hold on my behalf, we are at war, after all."

Men and women bowed and left to their various jobs within the maze. Ahun approached. "No word yet from Ukzahg, so we will continue our push forward." He fell silent as gunshots went off in the distance. "Our enemies are typical Orcs, fighting with simple firearms and blades of various styles."

I nodded. "How many injured?"

Ahun shook his head "I haven't gotten the numbers yet from Colonel Helesia today, but he and his men have been busy." He gestured and we started to follow into the maze. "I know his men will be beyond glad to have reinforcements."

"There should have been a caravan yesterday?" I asked, noting that he had said nothing of them yet.

He stopped, looking at me, emotion deep in his eyes. "They never arrived."

Civilians. The caravan was civilian doctors and nurses like ours. My heart lurched into my throat, but I set my jaw and stood strong.

"The Riders came just before sunset," he continued, "with a total of seven dragons and riders. I had them fan out to await the arrival of your caravan."

"How far our are we from Hastengrad?"

"From here, probably a seven hour drive if we could go straight, ten with the forests and swamps." He scratched his chin in thought. "A dragon, if willing to carry us, could probably get us there within two or three hours."

We continued walking, my bags felt even heavier than I knew they were on my already sore shoulders, making my side scream in pain. I was overdue for another dose of medication. I pushed the pain aside as best I could and followed the High General.

"How close are our closest men?" I asked.

"They've been fighting hard, and have been met with hard resistance. I have men two hours from here, though we often find opposition finding their way closer."

"How many times have you sent word to Ukzahg, and in which official channels?"

"Once a day, through all means that would ensure my qualifications to request such a fight."

I shook my head. "And still he refuses? Allowing his men to die along the way. Madness."

Ahun shrugged. "I know Ukzahg, he knows me. Or, at least, we once knew each other. He knows I have always been the better fighter, so he will postpone the Right by Combat until he has no other option."

That stopped me in my tracks. "You two knew each other?"

He nodded, smiling at an old memory. "Aye, we grew up in the same little coastal town, far north from here. He was bigger than me until I grew tired of being the small one."

"So you're not surprised he's hesitating?"

He let out a hearty laugh. "It's an Orc thing. He will send as many men that are willing to go, and they, wanting fame and glory in battle, will fling themselves upon our weaponry more in hopes of an honorable death than in trying to push us back."

"Fodder to keep his own soul safe." I muttered under my breath.

"Contact!" Someone shouted from the North. Gunfire thundered in the air. A shadow took out the sun for but an instant and a heavy gust of wind threatened to knock us down. Looking up I saw a blue dragon speed overhead, and felt the flames as it cleared the north wall.

I could feel the flames from the other side of the encampment.

I stood there, watching North as screams came into hearing for a fateful few seconds before withering away. "Clear!" Came the call before the momentary silence returned to the sounds of camp life.

The dragon flew back overhead, though this time it arched around the camp issuing a triumphant bellow.

"Remind me, should the need ever arise, to never make a Dragon Rider angry at me." Kutz said, his eyes as wide as mine.

"Aye lad, I felt the heat 'ere, past walls and distance." Kronda was shaking his head. "I don't think even my thick skull could survive that."

"No one could." I looked down, feeling an odd lack of emotions, a vast emptiness. "It is why dragons are feared. I cannot imagine what it would take to become a Rider."

"I have seen the training needed." Ahun cut in. "Needless to say it's an average of maybe ten percent of survivors actually are chosen by a dragon."

"Hear that folks," I glanced around at my crew, eyes pausing at Kutz and Hans, "be nice to the dragons and no trying to ride."

"Yes Sir." Came a myriad of replies.

"Let us continue to your barracks then I will show the doctors and nurses to the med bay while those guards who will be taking later shifts can rest." Ahun said, shrugging at the last bit. "Though most everyone here is a guard in one way or another so direct bodyguards might be a little over the top."

"They pretend to listen to me." I joked, giving Kutz a friendly shove which he quickly returned. "I don't think I have much control over them."

"Not one bit." Kutz laughed. "Heck you couldn't even keep us away from you when we were on leave!"

"And I got an earful about that so next time you're told to go home and rest, go home and rest."

"Aye, and stay out of my way." Kronda added in.

Silence fell over our group as more gunfire was heard in the distance.

"They're pretty close today." Ahun noted.

"Are they normally not?"

He shook his head. "Most days I can go without hearing a single round. They must have seen the dragons and decided to attack en force. It should thin them out significantly and allow us to move forward faster."

"Orc, what's yer plan on moving this whole camp closer to the goal?" Kronda asked.

Ahun turned, glaring at the Dwarf. "While you are here you will refer to me as High General, is that clear?" He waited for Kronda to nod before continuing. "That's the point of the maze-like construction of the camp. It's not really a maze, but rather a series of square clearings each with one or two spots in the wall open. When we have no opposition firing at us we can drop a whole section, load up, secure the opening to the rest of the encampment, and move that section to our next closest camp all within four hours."

"Impressive." Fitz whispered.

"We're not ready to move the med bay, that will be one of the last sections to move alongside the med staff barracks." He turned away from our group, turning down another path. "Lord Bubbles, we have a tent set aside for you and your personal guards close to my own."

"Thank you, High General, but please, while I'm here just call me Doctor Stan. I don't need special titles or any of that here."

He nodded. "That will sit better with the men."

Ahun paused outside a tent, a slumbering red dragon painted on a sign on the door. "Doctor Stan, you and your guards can leave your bags in here and continue on with the rest of us."

Inside the tent was scarcely furnished, three bunk beds and one slightly larger cot was set alongside one wall. Large chests sat open and empty at the foot of the beds, ready for our bags. There was a small table surrounded by chairs and a small kitchenette opposite the beds. A small wood stove was by the center pole, exhaust pipe going up and out, a pile of wood was behind it.

Aelyr chuckled. "Going all out for you, Sir, though I do think that High General Ahun's tent would be better furnished, at least with a desk and maybe two rooms."

"That's fine, Aelyr." I said, dropping the larger of the two bags into the chest and centering the full med pack backpack on my back. "I said I don't want to be treated special, but I also know that me being here is a significant morale booster so the soldiers will want some show."

Everyone agreed as they dropped bags and started heading back out the door.

Our next stop was the barracks for the medical staff. From the outside I couldn't see how they were set up though I noted a smoke pipe coming from the top of each. I was glad that no one was going to be cold if the temperature dropped at night.

From there we moved to the medical bay itself. It was a series of large pavilions, multiple smoke pipes coming from each one. Each was labeled with the intended purpose from Operations to Recovery.

An Elf had just backed out of the Operations tent, rankings of a Colonel sitting on his shoulders, roughly stitched to his doctors coat, bright red staining the front. Helesia was stitched equally as rough across his breast.

Colonel Helesia was tall and muscular, even in the ways of the normally tall and thin elves. His eyes were golden, his hair white but had a golden sheen in the light, and his skin had an unnatural glow.

"Never in my life did I want to go home with another man as much as I do Colonel Helasia." I heard Kutz say under his breath.

His comment was followed by agreement of everyone with us. I know I felt jealous at his beauty.

Colonel Helesia saluted to High General Ahun and made his way over. "Everyone is moving to Recovery, save two who are in the ICU section for observation and six that were lost on the table." Weariness was obvious in his silky smooth voice. "Those six, coupled with the twenty five that came in already gone from this world brings todays losses to thirty-one." He glanced over to us, eyes glinting in the light, but no emotion showed in them. "I am assuming these are my reinforcements?"

Ahun glanced at me, I nodded slightly for him to continue. I wanted to watch for now, to get a good idea of how this Elf worked with others.

"Most of them, yes, There are six guards in the mix." The Orc paused until Helesia looked him in the eyes. "There was supposed to be more in yesterday afternoon. They never made it."

Sadness flashed but for an instant in those golden eyes. So he did feel emotion, but had seen enough death out here that emotions did not hold much sway in his mind. I also saw a quick hint of irritation. "What am I to do with guards?" He snarled.

Ahun laughed. "They're not for you, don't fret. They'll stay out of the way and will help open doors." He glanced to the six behind me.

Aelyr puffed up. "Of course, here to help."

"See?" Ahun gestured with a hand.

Helesia rubbed the bridge of his nose with elegantly long fingers. "I know men of the Guard, they do not merely open doors for anyone. Why do I have six of them."

Ahun looked to me, pleading for help in his gaze. I stepped forward. "They're here for me, Colonel Helesia."

The Elf pinned me in his glare. I saw those metallic eyes matte over, losing their sheen. He was aura gazing. I could feel auras with close contact, and even see clouds of them in the contact, but few could physically see the mystical air around a person whenever they chose. What kind of Elf was he? I had never seen his type before.

"I do not know you, but you seem of a good sort of folk. Let me guess, private physician to the Lord Bubbles?" He glanced over my shoulder where the red cross behind a dragon stood clearly.

Ahun burst out laughing. He doubled over, trying not to fall on his side. Watching him made my own side hurt more, but I smiled awkwardly as he almost collapsed in the hysterical fit.

Helesia, finally, had an open show of irritation. "I do not see what is so funny, High General."

Kutz leaned over to me and whispered in my ear. "Should I tell him."

I shook my head, a smile coming to my own face. "Nah, either he'll figure it out or Ahun will regain sanity and tell him."

Helesia threw up his arms in defeat and we resigned to wait until Ahun had recovered.

"Colonel, my apologies, but this IS the Lord Stan Bubbles of Farysha." The glowing skin of the Elf turned a few shades pink. He turned back to me and bowed.

"I have made a wrong assumption. I had assumed it was a rumor started to boost morale."

I shook my head, still chuckling quietly though my ribs wished that I would stop. "No harm done, please, no need to bow or do any formalities here."

He straightened and nodded. "As you wish. Why, may I ask, are you here? To see our operation first-hand?"

"I came to help."

"Stan 'ere was one of the finest emergency room doctors we had, up until Farysha had greater need of him than we did." Kronda said, giving my hip a small shove.

I smiled down at him. "And now they're stuck with a doctor that needs a stepstool to talk to his patients."

He laughed heartily. "Ya ain't wrong!" He took a deep breath and calmed. "We do miss ya though, something fierce."

My heart ached. "I've missed you all too, Kronda. A decade of work there isn't something you can just walk away from."

"If you two would mind you can take your relationship elsewhere." Helesia interrupted. "For now we each need our rest. A Private will come and summon any who is needed. Guards, if the Lord is summoned for duty please make sure you stay OUT OF THE WAY." The Elf yelled through gritted teeth, I sensed a bit of magic making his voice louder. Aelyr winced as well. "Open doors, hold items, you are effectively nurses when we're at work. Understand?"

"Understood!" They each shouted.

"Good, off to bed, the lot of you." Colonel Helesia stalked off in the direction we came. His tent must me near mine.

"He gets like that." Ahun said once Helesia was out of earshot. "Don't let him wear you down."

"We all expect the best, and find any loss of life to be unacceptable." I noted, my eyes never having left the direction the man had walked off in. "It is nothing new to me, though he has seen vastly more." I turned my gaze to Ahun. "Magic user?"

He nodded. "One of the few we have. Light Elf to boot, though he prefers claiming he's a Sun Elf. Very powerful, even in combat with his magic."

"One more person to not piss off." I muttered before glancing around at my little group. "In any case, however, he is right. We need to get our rest before the next wave of patients comes in."

With a wave of nods, and a few yawns, we headed back to our bunks to undress, organize our items, and rest until we were needed.

TWENTY TWO

Dawn hadn't even touched the sky when a sharp knock at our door woke us up. Josh was already awake, having chosen to take up his usual night shift, so he set his reading tablet aside, took up his candle and opened the door.

A young man with glasses poked his head in. "Casualties, the doctor is needed in Operations."

I had already sat up, rubbing the sleep from my eyes as I dug out my Vycin. "On it."

He stared at me for a moment before nodding. "Sorry there's no time for coffee, sir. But it's urgent. I need to go wake the others, please report to Colonel Helesia."

He saluted quickly before turning around and leaving, letting the framed door close behind him with a soft slam.

Before I could finish getting dressed Josh had whipped up some instant coffee from what he found in the kitchenette setup. Apparently Ahun had thought ahead. I clipped my belt on, opting to unhook the sword, tossed my large med bag on my back, grabbed the lukewarm cup of coffee, and was out the door with Aelyr and Kutz on my heels in under fifteen minutes.

The medical area was already swarming with people. Overhead a pair of dragons, one with golden scales which was missing a limb and the smaller blue one we had seen yesterday, flew to the other side of the med bay wall. Together they reached over the wall and gently deposited injured men on liters to nurses and attendants waiting with gurneys.

Instead of gawking I dove into the fray towards the Operations tent. Once there Aelyr and Kutz took to opening doors, freeing up multiple nurses each and noticeably speeding up how fast soldiers were being treated.

A pair of nurses pulled me over to a wash station and helped sanitize me, putting a mask on my face and a cap over my hair as I scrubbed up. I was then led to the main part of the tent where any normal person would see disarray.

I was not normal.

Those with lesser injuries that needed treatment but were not necessarily life threatening were up front, nurses tending to each, while those needing full surgery or arteries stitched up were further back as they would be in the tent longer than the constantly rotating front.

As I was led to the back area I spread my aura to read those I passed. I stopped by one man who was complaining about a weird pain in his side. "Take him in the back." I said.

The nurse by his side laughed. "Just a small wound in the side, nothing major hit, just needs some stitches."

I shook my head. "The bullet bounced around, he has internal bleeding and a rip in his kidneys." I glowered at her.

She stopped what she was doing and glared at me. "And how would you possibly know that?"

I turned my aura on her, increasing the heat of her own to give my words the effect that I needed in order to save this mans life. "A man with the same talents as Colonel Helesia."

She paled and rose, wheeling the man away to double check on my words and to ensure he got the proper help he needed.

I continued on my path towards the back where I was needed, no one else had been misdiagnosed.

Most of the injuries I dealt with with was pulling out bullet fragments, massive cuts from edged weapons in areas the body armor just couldn't protect, and other lacerations that hit the arteries.

Most of these injuries I had seen before and treated, especially whenever a riot was drummed up in Hykur.

I had never worked quite at this speed, or on so many who needed help, however. I just remember the focus, barely noticing those around me. Just standing in one spot and nurses bringing men in and taking them out, cleaning me up again and again between each patient.

There were some I couldn't save, even with my magic assisting me. Five of them had injuries to their lung cavities, holes that not even my aura could hold close as they were too big. Three had ricochet through their intestines, having fractured or even shattered pelvic bones as well.

Those were the ones that made it to me with a heartbeat.

My morning continued as such, turning into day. It was over as suddenly as it began, though less chaotic, overbearingly quiet. Slowly I sat on the stool besides me, only now noting the stench in the air, mixed with the smells of cleaners trying to sanitize as much as they possibly could.

I felt sickened, this was the best military medical equipment my family had spared the budget for? This is how they wanted there men taken care of?

One more thing I needed to change.

I felt the aura of Colonel Helesia before he reached me, though I still jumped slightly when he touched my shoulder from behind.

"Easy there." He said softly.

I nodded as I stood and turned to face him. "Sorry, I know I'm only two weeks out of practice, but it feels like it was a lifetime ago."

"In a way it was." He crossed his arms over his chest. "You did good today. Go rest and take care of your ribs."

"Sounds like a good plan." Slowly I stood, trying to keep from twisting my side.

He stood in thought a moment. "You've studied magical application within the medical fields?"

"Seemed like the thing to do at the time."

He didn't say a word, just looked me over before turning. "Go take care of your ribs. We don't know when the next round of patients will be in. Freshly bleached coats will be at your tent shortly, make sure your patches are all moved over with haste." With that the Colonel walked away.

I followed him out the door where Aelyr and Kutz joined me, both of them yawning.

In silence we walked to our tent, me sliding out of the coat along the way. Hans opened the door, Josh was on his bunk snoring loudly. Aelyr and Kutz collapsed onto theirs, staring up at the bottom of the bunk above their heads.

Grüdar was sitting at the table, poking the woodgrain pressed into the plywood. "Lunch should be soon if anyone wanted to go eat."

"Let me shower first, then I'll go. If anyone wants to go first, please, don't wait." I said, sitting down and pulling out a knife.

Hans watched me as I cut the threads holding the patches onto the coat and deposit them on the table. I set the stained coat next to them and looked around the tent. "Anyone drop off more coats today?"

"Not yet," Grüdar responded, "they'll probably be in at some point soon if you need to transfer the patches."

I picked one up, my name patch, and turned it around. "Why isn't this loopstrap if we keep needing to move the patches from one thing to another?"

Aelyr laughed in his bunk. "Maybe your predecessors didn't care much about military budget."

"Well," I tossed the patch back down and walked to my chest, pulling on the uniform I was to wear around camp when I'm not working, "then remind me, when we get back, to change that. We should have the budget now that certain stupid things are cut out of it."

"Like all that porn?" Kutz called, not moving nor opening his eyes.

That made me wince. "Ugh, yes. Just that could probably pay for half of the military forces to get their badges loopstrap backings." I had thankfully forgotten about that, I glared at Kutz, though he wouldn't notice.

"If you're chatting I'd like to go get food." Hans said as I made sure I was squared away.

"All right, all those who want to eat let's go." I snagged my bottle of Vycin and shoved in it a pocket.

Aelyr and Kutz both groaned but didn't move. I stood by the doorframe with Hans, Fitz, and Grüdar. "Come on you two, if I can get up and move for food then so can you."

Aelyr sat up but Kutz remained where he was, groaning obnoxiously loudly.

"Kutz," I drew out his name, "who here has broken ribs?"

"You...."

"Who had to work all day saving lives while you opened doors?"

"....you...."

"Who is starving to death and will go eat but wants to make sure those that chose to come with him instead of staying at the Pagoda to watch over the Princess get to eat too?"

Kutz opened an eye to glare at me as he sat up. "Fine."

Aelyr tapped my shoulder. "We did to more than just open doors, just so you are aware, sir. We helped in any way we could, especially when patients needed to be lifted and moved."

I winked at him. "I assumed as much, I just wanted to make sure that even Kutz got food in him and didn't starve."

Aelyr smiled. "That's why we like you and chose to make sure you didn't do something stupid and get yourself killed."

"That is easy to do out here." Hans noted.

"Kutz!" Fitz called. "Hurry up!"

Kutz stumbled over to us, stretching and yawning. "I'm here, I'm here."

Together we walked to the Officers Lounge, grabbed trays of food, and sat down in silence. No one else save a cook was in the tent. Kutz ate about half his tray before passing out facedown in his food. Aelyr pulled him off his tray but chose to not wipe anything off his face. Once we ere full we returned to our tent, leaving Kutz snoring in the lounge. We did try to wake him up, but even Grüdar didn't want to carry him back. I was sure I'd hear it from Ahun later.

Hans, Fitz, and Grüdar stayed up while Aelyr and myself passed out, the shower I wanted to take completely gone from my mind.

TWENTY THREE

I dreamt of the men I failed to save. They kept looking at me, their pale eyes confused, pleading while I worked on others. I kept trying to return, to save them, bring them back to us, but those who were still alive and fading were being rolled before me, nurses whose faces I couldn't see blocking my way around them.

I woke up in a cold sweat, bolting upright and grasping at my aching side. I took a moment to reestablish the strength of my aura around my ribs, using it to check for how well they're healing, hold them in place, and nullify the pain somewhat until I could take my next dosage of medication.

Once that was done I looked around. It was still dark. Josh was sitting at the table next to a low candle, reading something on an electronic tablet.

"Did someone come to gather us?" I asked, my voice barely audible.

Josh looked up, his curly brown hair bouncing slightly. "No, not yet at least."

I walked over to the stack of boxes that made up the cabinet and pulled out a protein bar and a bottle of water. I sat down at the table opposite Josh and took my medication.

"Why are you up?"

He shrugged. "Used to staying up late, surprised Grüdar hasn't been staying up too." He set the tablet down. "Also figured someone should keep a night watch in case there's another assassination attempt."

I nodded, he did have a good point. We didn't know if the Dragon Talon had infiltrated the Military yet or were just pulling from veterans.

"What have you been doing for food?"

He smiled. "Those that stay here while you're working have been stashing some in the mini fridge for me. It's not much, but it's better than just protein bars and those ready to eat meal packs."

"Of which we have plenty." I jabbed my thumb over my shoulder to the boxes labeled R.E.M. sitting in a corner.

"You should go back to sleep, Sir." Josh said, looking at the candle. "We're not sure when you'll be called to save lives again, you need your rest."

I cast my eyes down, picking at a point in the plywood table. "Save lives or watch helplessly as children die under my hands while I'm trying to patch more holes than cheese?"

Josh remained quiet, flicking a finger through the flame of the candle. After a moment he got up and tossed a couple more logs into the warm stove in the center of the tent, checked a pot of water on top, and returned to his seat.

"Sir, you can't save everyone." He didn't look at me, "When the Gods will it then it is their time. Not before, not after."

I gritted my teeth. "The Gods be damned, these are children."

"They're adults, just young ones, or else they wouldn't be allowed to join up and fight." Josh leaned over the table, "Think of how Ûlfin must have felt knowing you were coming here. He's gotta be what, hundred and fifty years old by now? You're thirty-eight? The new young Lord with no heirs leaves his fiance to go fight?"

I relaxed, resigning myself to open my water and snack. "You do have a point."

He leaned back in his chair. "We all do what we think is right." He shrugged. "Well, for the most part we do. Shit happens, sometimes it's good, and sometimes it's bad. But it's usually out of our control, so there's no reason to beat ourselves up over it."

I let silence fall as I ate the chocolatey bar that was more chalk than chocolate and peanut butter. I chased it down with two pills and a drink of water.

Why have magic if I can't do anything more? I thought, still unable to get the nightmare from my mind. *There has to be a way.*

Josh continued to watch me, concern in his eyes. "Go back to bed, sir, you'll be happy you slept more when you're needed."

I sighed deeply. "You're probably right."

He nodded slowly and picked his tablet back up.

"What are you reading?"

He shrugged. "Some book about a magic horse my wife asked me to read."

I raised an eyebrow. "Are you liking it?"

"I'm only a few chapters in, but it's not bad. But it's the first book in her favorite series so it'll be something we can talk about together when I get home."

"Sounds, quite nice actually." I smiled as I stood and returned to my bunk. "Sleep well, Josh, when you get a chance."

"Hope your dreams are nicer to you, sir."

I lay down, watching the canvas roof above me flex under the tension of the cold wind. I was beyond thankful there was a heater keeping it above freezing in the tent. I thought about Aleyna, if she had any books she thought I should read.

With the wind howling around us I drifted back to sleep. This time, no faces haunted my rest.

* * *

We woke again when the diluted sun shone through the rooftop. I curled up under my wool blanket, not wanting to get up.

In the distance I heard a horn call awake soldiers still sleeping. I knew that doctors were getting special treatment, as is we were stationed further away so that the horn wouldn't bother us.

"We should go eat." Kutz suggested.

"I'll come with today." Josh yawned.

I grumbled something but didn't move.

"What was that, sir?" Kutz asked me. "I couldn't hear you under that blanket."

I lifted a small section up to glare at the cheerful man a moment before plopping the blanket back down on my face.

Grüdar chuckled deeply. "I don't think he speaks glare."

"Nope!" Kutz agreed. "Just common. I mean, I guess I can try other languages but they'll just come out as gibberish."

"Please do not try, at least Elvish." Aelyr asked.

"Let's give the Lord a small break, guys." Josh said. "He woke up before sunrise and passed back out."

"Jooossshhhh," Kutz dragged out the name, "you're awake, I'm awake, the Elf and Orc are awake, heeeee can be awake tooooo."

Someone sat down on my bed, the aura matched the feeling of Aelyrs'. "Don't think you're getting out of this." He said softly. "Besides," he added to Kutz, "I'm only half-Elf."

"Fiiiiiiiiiine." I dragged the word out as long as I possibly could as I flipped the blanket down and sat up. I looked around at everyone, stopping and raising an eyebrow at Kutz. "Pineapple jammies? Really?"

He stopped digging in his trunk and puffed out his chest in pride. "They are warm and comfy cozy and have matching booties and cap."

"You did miss the full spectacle that was Kutz waking up." Grüdar said over his shoulder.

The bantering went on as we got dressed and left to go eat, Kutz doing all he could to keep Josh awake, going as far as to threaten to leave his face in the bacon if he passes out on his food.

Breakfast was bacon, scrambled eggs, and hash. We all ate with haste, I was the only one not cracking jokes. Ahun stopped by our table on the way out, patting my shoulder and telling me that Colonel Helesia said that I was rather impressive. He had to return to his own tent to sign off on paperwork and get to his duties for the day.

The following days went as such. Casualties were low, apparently the arrival of the Riders scared off most of the enemy combatants. Little by little blocks of the camp were moved north, one a day. Everything seemed to close in and center around the command and medical blocks.

Almost a week into our stay, and one more rush of patients, Ahun moved the command block and one quarter the medical block to the Northern Camp, putting us two hours closer to our goal of Hastengrad. Colonel Helesia stayed behind with the bulk of the medics to use what remained of the camp as our main medical camp. He had orders to start pushing some of the camp a days ride south, so soldiers traveling between Farysha and Hastengrad would have somewhere to rest for the night. I went with my guards to assist the medical staff on the front lines with Ahun.

Even then things were oddly calm. A few Gremlin attacks caused a major rush of patients alongside a push by the Orcs every few days.

High General Ahun was convinced this meant that the High Chieftains' armies were thinning and that soon we should receive word that he accepted the invitation for Rule by Combat.

Every day Ahun sent the challenges. Every day the messenger returned empty handed. I was just glad Ukzahg didn't kill our messenger.

Every day we were able to push a little closer to Hastengrad. Ahun wanted to send the Riders out to destroy everything in our path and to walk to the capital in one day. I was ferociously against such an act. We weren't here to kill innocents, we were here to stop the deaths of many. And yet, even after two weeks of our forces constantly pushing closer to where Ukzahg was holed up, he refused the challenges. Further we pushed into the chill of winter in Paryda. There was no snow, but it got a little too close to freezing every night.

One day, in our tent, Kutz had taken to spreading himself out on the table to be funny. "I haaate this weather!" He complained. "Hot as balls during the day, cold as snow at night!"

"I haaaate," Aelyr responded, drawing out the word hate longer than Kutz did on purpose, "annoying humans that for some reason want to take up the table we eat off of."

Kutz stuck his tongue out at the half-Elf and rolled over, posing like a pinup model in uniform. "It's not like we eat off this table every day."

"I do." Josh said from his bunk.

Kutz stammered some incoherent response but got off the table.

"Clean it too." Josh grumbled as he rolled over onto his side.

Kutz huffed but started cleaning, much to the laughter of everyone else in the tent.

For the most part we spent the time learning more about each other. How Josh had taken so many night shifts that he has issues staying awake if there's any light. How Aelyrs father was a Moon Elf, but his human mother raised him to keep him from becoming an assassin. Hans and Josh were cousins, and Grüdar was Ûlfins' nephew, having joined up initially to spend more time with his uncle then falling in love with protecting people. Kutz was an orphan, and had taken to being a clown of sorts to help others smile, since he learned at a young age the true power behind a smile and a laugh.

Some of them, Aelyr and Grüdar to be specific, didn't need to be told about my family history as they had just started in the Penthouse when I was little. They had known my mother better than I had, and it was pleasing to talk about her.

They both missed her, and were glad that I had grown up to be more like her than my father. They also both were convinced my father had her murdered one day because she was too nice and was working on undermining some of the more draconian laws that Farysha had.

The thought that she was killed at my own fathers command did not surprise me, it was the type of man he was. I did wish I had more time with her than the short six years I had. It did, however, make me feel sick to my stomach.

Occasionally Ahun came in to spend time with us, when duties allowed. Him and Aelyr would tell stories on the differences between Sun and Moon Elves, and how all plain old Elves were a mixture between the two and you could tell by their eyes which family their blood belongs to.

Ahun would regale us on the days when he and Ûlfin were younger, after he had moved with his family to Farysha to avoid the constant war between clans which usually included the murdering of entire towns. The two had become tight friends, and with that friendship came a competition to be the better fighter, to rise through the ranks the highest. They still would argue over who has more power. I didn't have the heart to tell him that I had made Ûlfin my heir until such time that Aleyna and myself had a child.

That thought kept returning to me. That I was engaged to a Princess. That we would one day have children. I was terrified that I would be as bad a father as mine own. What would I even name a child?

Aelyr suggested Luna, Josh agreed. The Orcs kept saying I should just sit at my keyboard and type random letters until I came up with something I liked. I didn't think Aleyna would like that method very much.

And so the days turned into another week. No word from Ukzahg. Letters from us being sent home as we kept internet and electricity down to a minimum. Josh kept proving sneaky with his tablet and wind powered charger, though he had stocked it with about a hundred books. Kutz joked that Josh would read all of them before we received the acceptance letter from the High Chieftain.

We were there for three weeks, wherein Josh read about ten books, when that letter finally came in alongside an ornate war axe coated in dried blood.

TWENTY FOUR

"We leave tomorrow." Ahun said from behind his desk. "Just bring a single pack, make sure the six with you also only bring minimals."

"Understood." I exhaled. I'd be telling a lie if I said I wasn't nervous to the point of being unable to eat.

"Not asking if I'm ready?" The Orc asked, a smirk on his face.

I chuckled nervously. "Ready or not, this will all be decided soon."

"Day after tomorrow. Ukzahg needs to put us up for a night to ensure him and myself are properly rested for the fight."

"He doesn't have to include me in those preparations."

Ahun put a finger in the air. "He does, you and your men are part of my dedicated dozen."

"I don't understand."

He tapped the finger on his desk, thinking of how to explain the tradition. "Each side brings a dozen men to watch and judge the fight. Half of each fighters men watch him, the other half watch the other man. If any thinks that there is cheating going on, most of the men watching the fight must agree that the cheat happened for anything to be done. If cheating does occur, however, and the watchers lied about such then the watchers are summarily executed along with the offender. Basically just stand against the wall, stay quiet, and trust in me."

I ran my fingers through my hair. "So, don't make something up to try and give you the advantage."

Ahun smiled. "I already have the advantage. This may be where Ukzahg lives and trains, but he's thinking he's worn me down from this month of war." Suddenly he burst out in laughter. "I've been in battles longer than this and fought opponents twice his strength without breaking a sweat."

That did help me relax, though just a small bit. "No pressure but you do know what's on the line if you do happen to fail."

He grew serious as he looked at me. "Oh I do. H recognizes you at some point so I die, you die, your men die, and Faryshas military goes to Paryda. Or, at least Ukzahg believes so. My men have orders to fight to the death to return home and destroy everything in the process." His eyes blazed. "Ukzahg would have each man killed at his hands, no longer how long it took."

I tried a smile, it must have turned out awkward as Ahun brought back his smirk. "Yea, don't get me killed before I have a kid, sound good?"

He rocked back, his laughter booming. "So, once you have an heir I'll take you to where we train our elite forces in the Mountains." He leaned forward, a glint in his eye. "Want to fight a chimera with your bare hands?"

"NO!" I stammered, waving my hands back and forth. "I'm a doctor, not a fighter."

Slowly he nodded. "One day we'll need to teach you some things about self defense so you're at least a little harder to kill."

"I can fire a pistol?" I offered with a shrug.

"You need more than that." Ahun took a calming breath as he looked at the rough page on his desk.

"First let's get home, alright?"

"Sounds like a plan." He stood, stretching as he did so. "For now let's both rest. Tomorrow we have some traveling to do followed by a feast."

The thought of food made my stomach twist. "I'm not sure I can eat much."

"You won't have to." Ahun walked around his desk and started towards the door to his tent. "It's another formality."

Together we left the tent, men were moving with haste all around us. They had their orders to fight and retreat if Ahun fell. Their number one concern was to destroy everything that couldn't be taken with and to get everyone from Farysha home safe. Every man was starting preparations to leave in a rush if necessary.

And through it all Ahun didn't seem phased. He walked with his head high and confidence in his step.

We bid each other farewell and good night as I turned to my tent. Everyone was inside sitting at the table, watching the door. I felt fairly awkward as I came in to their eyes staring at me.

"Well?" Aelyr asked.

"Tomorrow we leave for Hastengrad. We are to watch Ukzahg for anything that might be cheating, but if we make anything up to give Ahun the advantage then we can kiss our asses goodbye."

"Don't cheat. Got it." Kutz said.

I nodded. "During the fight we will stand in a ring against the walls of the room. We will remain quiet and keep our eyes open. And if Ahun falls..."

"If the High General falls, so do we." Grüdar whispered.

I nodded that it was the truth. My jaw was too tight to say much more, not that I could with my heart thrumming in my throat and my stomach down by my feet.

Josh stood from the table first. "We won't abandon you, Stan. Not just because we swore oaths, but because we're friends here. Friends don't turn their backs on each other."

One by one the others stood and voiced their agreement.

Aelyr spoke last. "Stan, you know we'll fight and die to protect you, knowing full well that you would try to jump in the fray to keep us safe."

I let out a half-hearted chuckle. "That is the truth."

Aelyr smiled. "We even have it planned out!"

"What?"

They each looked super proud that they managed to foil imaginary me in a fight that hasn't even happened yet.

"Grüdar will knock you out so you can't cast spells, pick you up, and run off with you while the rest of us kick ass!" Aelyr said with pride, raising a fist in a mock punch.

I scratched the back of my head. "You guys really do have it planned out."

Grüdar could not have looked more proud. None of them could, really. It was a comfort to see everyone so sure in their abilities.

I went to the stove and started lighting the fire within. "Ok guys, we leave early in the morning, so let's all get sleep." I looked up at Josh. "You too, night owl."

"But when the Moon's awake I'M awake!" Josh mockingly whined, flopping about on his bunk, almost kicking Kutz.

Grüdar grunted a laugh. "Keep that humor when we are facing down a city full of swords and guns fighting for our lives with our bare hands."

Fitz looked over his bare shoulder, simple pajamas in hands. "You don't think Ahun will win?"

He paused. "I think he can, I also think Ukzahg will play dirty and his team will never call him on it. If we do and they don't we risk execution all the same."

"Then let's live as if they plan on ambushing and killing us anyway." I pulled my own sleeping shirt over my head. "Let's get a good night sleep, go to Hastengrad tomorrow, and pray to all the Gods in the Heavens that are heads remain on our shoulders instead of on pikes."

Nervous laughter surrounded me as we got dressed. It quickly fell into silence as the rest of us climbed into our bunks.

I couldn't sleep. By the rustling I heard no one else could either.

In the silence, with the light of the soon to be full moon glowing through the canvas, a voice filled the air in song.

Kutz was singing.

It was a ballad somewhere between a dirge and a lullaby. It was a song of goodbyes.

Hans and Fitz joined in, Aelyr started adding another song of the same tune and tempo but in Elvish.

I listened, sadness welling up in me, though it was different than that which I had felt before. This wasn't the sadness that follows death. This was the before. Knowing tonight could very well be our last. That tomorrow could be an ugly ambush, that we might not even make it to the required rooms set aside for us.

The lyrics Kutz spoke were a story telling of a farmer well loved by the fairest in the land, who had been called to war for a greedy King. Every day he wrote, but never did a letter come to him. Every day for ten years he fought, and gained new injuries alongside great renown. One day, the war was over, and the great hero was finally able to return home to his family.

But they were not there, the lowly King who refused to fight with his own troops had murdered his childrenand livestrock, salted his fields, and taken his wife as his own shortly after the war began. The whole confrontation had been a farce.

Scorned, the hero rose up against the King, bringing his allies from the battles with him. Together they stormed the castle, hoping to bring down the tyrant and free the heros wife.

Sadly, the men were outnumbered and worn from battle while the Kings guards were freshly rested, having remained in the castle during the war. While the hero did find a way to sneak into the castle, the fight met them before they could get to his wife.

The batle was long and bloody. Each man the hero brought with him took ten of the Kings Guard down with him, the hero took fifty on his own. Finally, the hero himself fell at the hands of the King in a final bought, fought for the Crown before his fair wife.

The tune shifted to something slower, deeper. Kutz was the only one singing at this point, even Aelyr stopped his Elvish harmony.

The story continued with the heros widow, forced to become Queen by the greedy King, slipping poisons into his drink to avenge the hero, before passing in her sleep of a broken heart as she mourned her lost family, knowing that what remained of the Guard would do far worse to her should they learn of her assassination of the King.

The song ended with the family reuniting in the Silver Halls of the Moon in the Heavens. Their souls remaining together for eternity.

The silence after the song was worse than it was beforehand. I would love to say that I drifted off to sleep before the verses regarding the fighting, but I couldn't, no one could.

And so we stayed awake, watching for the new day, worried about the fate of our lives and of Farysha itself.

TWENTY FIVE

As we traveled north to Hastengrad the terrain smoothed out, turning from swamps to thick pine forests. The dawn came and the sun rose in the sky. We sat alongside six others and High General Ahun in the back of a transport truck with our day packs between our knees. We watched the countryside go by through the open windows, the canvas rolled up so we could see.

No one said a word.

Ahun sat focused, more than likely running everything he knows of Ukzahg through his head.

I know I was running through all the ways I could die today and tomorrow, much less in regards to going home in any case. I wondered if Aleyna would be upset at my passing, her father probably would be. Hope and Sera I knew would be devastated.

Letters had been given to us as we loaded up. My guards each had letters clasped in their hands from their wives and children. Hope, Sera, and Aleyna had sent letters to me. Hope and Sera had wondered if I was well and wished me good luck in our endeavors.

Aleyna had sent an update every day on goings on of the Pagoda and Hykur. Thankfully nothing bad had been going on, and all those who worked in the Pagoda seemed excited in regards to our pending wedding. She hoped that the Riders were assisting in all regards, adding that the Bisnian forces are ready to assist if necessary.

I hoped that they weren't needed. That tomorrow morning Ahun won and we could go home. There were so many ifs. So much that can go right, or go wrong.

Aelyr was scribbling away on a letter to his own wife. The others either stared at their letters or out the windows.

I watched them. Every one of them. I watched their faces, focused on how they were, who they were. I wanted to make sure I remembered them if I so happened to make it home alive and they stayed back and lost their lives to defend me.

Through the entire trip I could not shake an overwhelming feeling of dread. I was probably being over paranoid, Ahun seemed confident in his abilities.

But it had been years since he last saw Ukzahg, and many things can change over that course of time.

As the sun rose to the center of the sky we reached the capital city of Paryda.

Hastengrad was not a typical city. Houses were more like cabins, each spread out and deep on their land behind trees and fields. The larger the homes became the more they looked like ships turned upside down, using the hull as a roof. I could swear some were once ships, dried barnacles speckling the wood.

The home of the High Chieftain was large, at least three stories tall, and impressively long, tapering down to a single story at the ends. Our truck pulled up near the ornately carved double doors that served as the entrance. The doors were open, and a sleek young Orc maiden was standing in the doorway, awaiting us.

Ahun lead our small party as the driver was given directions on where to park the transport. I fell in a step behind him. Normally it would be the other way around, however, we needed Ahun to fight, not me. There was a chance the Orcs would request me to fight if I assumed leadership.

The maiden bowed at our approach. "Greetings, Master Ahun and company."

He bowed as well, we followed suit. "Shield Maiden. I was expecting Master Ukzahg."

"The High Chieftain will meet you tomorrow in the ring." She smiled at the larger Orc. "Tonight he is in his chambers, meditating."

I could see Ahuns' jaw twitch, but he nodded. "He is master of this house, if it is his wish to remain in his chambers then that is his right."

The maiden seemed pleased at the response. She stepped aside and ushered us inside. "Then please, enter as guest."

The entryway to the hall reminded me of a hunting lodge. Great animals stood stuffed along the walls, hanging on plaques or standing upon detailed mounts. Carved pillars held the roof up, two stories above our heads stood open to the room, railings keeping people from falling over accidentally. A throne sat on a dais at the far end of the room. Tables stood on either side of large fire pits, boars and stags hung on rotisseries being basted by more lovely Orcish ladies filled the room with a delicious smell.

The scent turned my stomach sour, I was too nervous to eat.

The maiden came to the front of our party and bowed again. "Please, take your ease and eat. You have the entirety of the second floor to the right," she gestured with a jeweled hand, "for your rest. Should you desire company we can... aquire... that which you desire." She added with a sly smile. "The ring will be prepared at dawn in front of this home, please do not be late."

Ahun bowed respectfully. "We will not be."

She nodded quickly and walked off, a slight bounce in her step as she left towards the left wing of the building.

We sat and food was brought to us, large bowls of fruits, platters of breads, and boards piled high with meats, cheeses, and other spreads.

Everyone picked at their food rather than digging in to enjoy the feast. Other Orcs that lived or worked came and ate with gusto. Ahun ate well, but did not indulge. He even turned down the offer of mead.

We stayed in the hall for a few hours, barely speaking, barely eating, and looking around with blank eyes. I knew if we survived tomorrow we'd be looking around at the carvings in wonder, but right now we were far too worried.

But we ate, making sure we weren't going through the day on empty. Each of us added more on our plates to take to our rooms so we could snack throughout the day.

"So, meditating?" Kutz finally asked. "Is that something he normally does."

Ahun chuckled. "He's not meditating in the way you think." He set his fork down and leaned forward to whisper. "He can be very much the same way as our former Lord was."

Kutz spat his drink out all over the table and Fitz. "Hey!!"

"Sorry." Kutz shrugged.

Ahun wore a sly smile. "He can do as he wishes. I assume he has a small feast as well in his chambers for him and those helping him meditate. The more he wears himself out, the easier tomorrow will be."

I relaxed some, if Ukzahg was keeping himself up and active then we had a far better chance of Ahun winning. Suddenly I was starving, so I allowed myself to eat more.

Our champion smiled when he saw me suddenly stuff a huge chunk of roast boar in my mouth.

"Trust me, Stan." He said, not using my titles as agreed. We assumed Ukzahg would react negatively to my presence.

I swallowed. "I do. I've already seen so much bad, I'm worried about more bad happening."

"Not tomorrow. Tomorrow we feast. Tomorrow I sit upon that throne." He smiled viciously. "Tomorrow we win."

"You know that he will recognize me tomorrow."

He nodded. "Ideally he will realize what's going on and will allow you to remain. He can't refuse you after officially offering hospitality to you. Under the same laws he cannot kill you unless I fall."

Ahun leaned over to me. "He is fighting to prove a point and because his advisors are making him. Had we fought our way here I would have automatically been given the throne as he would have been seen as a coward. I," he pointed to his chest, "am fighting for more than me. I am fighting for the first leader I've cared about, for his life, and to beat down an unruly child who has stepped out of place once again." I felt like there was more that he wasn't adding on. I didn't push him for it, it woud be revealed tomorrow.

He rocked back in his chair, folding his arms. "This is something I should have done a long, long time ago."

"Something you should have done?" Hans asked.

Ahun nodded. "Only one walks off the list. Ukzahg was better at gaining alliances than myself. His family friends disliked my own family, they were the reason we moved to Farysha." He slammed a fist down on the table. "I had returned, at his request, quite often to train together. Had I sent the challenge when he first got uppity like the child he is, then this would not be happening now."

"Or," I pointed out, "you'd be fighting someone far stronger, or even for them instead of Farysha."

He lifted a glass in agreement before taking a sip of the golden liquid within.

We spent time just talking about whatever came to mind. My guards enjoyed gossiping about different dignitaries and how they treated each other at formal get togethers at the Pagoda. I only remembered attending a few of them, and I did hope I would get to enjoy more.

I'm not certain how much time passed as we sat, ate, and talked. We started eating off the plates we had packed to take to our rooms. Eventually we refilled the plates and walked across the hall and found the stairs to the next floor.

The hallways were as equally ornate as the feasting hall. The rooms matched. Each had different trophies hanging on the walls with soft firelight illuminating the wooden walls and decor. We chose rooms near the end of the hall. Each only had a single bed, so Ahun and I took the furthest rooms with my guards next to us and the remaining watchers down from them.

For the first time in almost a month I saw myself in a mirror. I had the start of a beard, the dark stubble matching my black hair despite attempts to shave. I was tanner as well, no longer the exceedingly pale of only being outside to travel to and from work.

The overall darker complexion served to draw a sort of dangerous complexion to my eyes, making them pop more than normal. I tested a few expressions, the glower especially had gained power.

I noticed a few new wrinkles as well, and was that a gray hair? All within the short time I've been Lord of Farysha. I plucked the pale hair from my head and glanced around to ensure no one snuck into my room to see it.

I felt like I looked more like a Lord now than a doctor. It felt awkward looking at a face I didn't fully recognize, and knowing that it was the new me. I tried to imagine this new face in a dark suit, a glimmering Collar of Estate on his shoulders, official white belt bearing the Sword of State opposite an elegant drop holster for his sidearm.

I felt like the imaginary me was someone I would feel alright with becoming.

I smiled, turning from the mirror and dropping my bag on a chair by a small side table. The cloth sack attached to one side thunked against the table and stood out awkwardly. I untied it and set up on the table itself. The sak held my white belt with blade and pistol safe within. I ran my fingers over the surface, still worried, but not as much as this morning. I undressed, donning my pajamas with a sleepy haste. I was eager to sleep in an actual bed.

I was eager to be home. To spend time with Aleyna. To hug my cat. To feel safe.

I knew Ahun was confident. He asked me to trust him, so I did. I just hoped and prayed that Ukzahg didn't have any schemes planned.

I looked at the sconces on the wall, they were not actual flame but rather a set up similar to that which I used in my own bedroom. Looking around I found the main light switch hidden as a branch against the wooden walls.

Turning off the lights I turned and stumbled to the bed, stubbing my toes a few times in the process. Finding the soft surface I clambered up and in.

The bed was large and plush, covered with furs from various animals. I wasn't sure how well this building was heated, seeing it's more medieval build, but I was warm all the same and the furs would help if the temperature dropped too much.

I didn't smile in the dark of the room, but I did relax.

Sleep came to us all without any issues. We felt more confident in regards to tomorrows fight, and in our moment of relaxation our exhaustion caught up to us.

I had dreams of Ahun failing, of Ukzahg slicing my throat and dropping me to slowly die with Ahuns' dead eyes watching, of Aleyna in mourning for her lost fiance.

I dreamt of Farysha falling.

TWENTY SIX

Dawn came before we realized it.

The same Orc maiden from last night came and woke up the watchers down the hall who, in turn, woke the rest of us.

We were told to continue wearing what we had, and so we did. Ahun, on the other hand, came out of his room wearing a bearskin robe made of multiple bears so as not to look cartoonishly tiny on him. The head of the largest of the pelts sat on his head akin to a helmet, the arms going down around his like half-finished sleeves.

I was unsure if he wore anything underneath as I could only see his bare feet and calves plodding along on the carpeted floors.

In silence we followed him down to the front doors. We exchanged nervous glances when we saw they were closed. The first of the morning light spread across the floor from lofty windows.

Ahun didn't pause or skip a step. He walked straight to the doors and pushed them open for a dramatic entrance.

Ropes tied to poles made up the combat ring. Torches stood atop each pole. A pedestal in the center held a pillow made of dark fur and a bleached white knife carved from bone, the blade of which was stained with layers of blood. A large crowd stood around the ring, parting for us.

Ukzahg stood next to the blade, watching our approach. A small, hunched figure in a dark cloak stood on the other side. I assumed that Orc would be the official judge.

As we fanned out according to directions I noted a ring of Orcs bearing both bearded axes and slinged rifles standing behind us.

Ahun noticed this as well. "Armed guards? That is grounds for a forfeit."

"He is correct." The figure, an elderly woman, said. "Disperse the guards or be considered a coward."

Ukzahg glared at Ahun before nodding and waving a hand. The men dispersed into the crowd.

Ahun eyed Ukzahg warily. "Matron Judge, in the case the men have not truly left and fell me before the Bone Knife, what occurs? I ask so that my Watchers know how to act accordingly."

The hood nodded. "A far question. You may name a second, should such a horror occur then the High Chieftain has forfeited his life, your second would claim the Bone Knife and take the title."

"Then I name Grüdar Flameheart as my second." He gestured to the Orc who had taken up a spot behind him.

Grüdar nodded his acceptance.

"Then it is settled." Matron Judge said. "Enter the ring, Challenger Ahun."

Ahun handed his robe back to Grüdar, revealing little but bare skin and simple, tight, black shorts. Ukzahg was dressed in a similar manner.

Together they placed their hands on the dagger, swearing an oath to fight fairly lest they be labeled a coward and cast shame upon their families.

Ukzahg scanned the crowd, specifically those of us Ahun brought with him, one more time as the dagger pedestal was removed. His eyes landed on me and his scowl deepened.

"Why is HE here?"

"He is trusted friend, I requested his presence." Ahun responded calmly.

I felt my heart begin to race.

Ukzahg spun to the Matron Judge. "I will not have this man here. He should be taken as prisoner of war. He....." He trailed off, watching his words. Apparently Martin was not considered a true heir despite being of hid blood and was not to be discussed as the child of the High Chieftain. "He murdered a trusted soldier before my eyes." He growled. She held up a frail hand. "You cannot request him to leave, he is a Watcher, and you had given him guest rights upon his arrival."

I felt a quic wave of relief wash through me. Had Ukzahg met us at the door as he was supposed to he would have killed me then and there.

Veins stood out on the Orcs forehead as he tried to figure out some way to see my death before the fight. As he realized he missed his chance last night. He gritted his teeth before he spoke again. "Then I at least expect him in chains, so that he does not pull any magic tricks during the battle, and cannot run away should I win and his rights expire." He growled.

The Matron Judge thought a moment before nodding. "I find this request acceptable, Challenger?"

Ahun thought a moment before glancing and me and nodding very slowly, adding, "Yes, but one of mine hold the keys should I win."

Ukzahg grudgingly agreed, glaring at me as he signaled at his guards. Silence settled over th field for but a few minutes before a slight clinking was heard coming from the Great Hall.

Fear grew as the sound of iron chains came closer. They looked as black, yet carried the sheen of ice and a few white specks of frost. My racing heart jumped into my throat and my stomach dropped. Witchers Chains. Used to inhibit the use of magic.

They weren't hard to make. One without talent in magic had to take iron in any combination of shapes, as long as they formed a completed circle around the neck and wrists of the intended wearer. From there, the iron must me thrown in fire then stored in a freezer, the combination of the two purifying the metal from any residual aura, and allowing it to nullify the aura of any who wore it.

A side effect would be that the wearer would be immune to magic and be invisible to those who use auras to see. Though, at the moment, I didn't really care about the side effects, I just didn't want to die.

I looked up to Ahun, I knew I couldn't keep the fear from my eyes, even if I could try to hide it from my face. Resolve shined in his eyes as he nodded again.

I trusted him. I had to.

I extended my shaking hands to the armed Orc before me. It sounded like they clanked close far louder than I know they did. A larger ring was locked around my neck, the chain looping lazily down to the one connecting my wrists.

Immediately my side began to ache and I felt an odd blindness to the world around me. The auras I had grown accustomed to sensing with every step were gone.

A chill settled deep into my core. I prayed to every God, to the Sleeping Dragon, to every spirit, that Ahun would win.

The guard stood besides me, resting a hand on my shoulder. Unless Ahun won I was not leaving Hastengrad alive. Aelyr stepped over to my other, taking the key from the man and resting a hand on my other shoulder.

The Matron Judge called for attention, and Ahun and Ukzahg met her in the middle of the field.

"You have both sworn oaths. Allow me to introduce the combatants to the crowd." She walked through the two of them, turning to look at those assembled before her.

"Ahun is the Challenger. He was born in a town on the North Coast, one which had been destroyed and stricken from record, the same of which Ukzahg hails from. He challenges not for himself, but as he feels that Ukzahg has overstepped his boundaries by calling for war against Farysha, sending our men, our husbands, our brothers, our fathers to die for a war that need not happen. It is his desire to remove a tyrant and return peace to the lands."

She gestured to Ukzahg. "High Chieftain Ukzahg is the one challenged. The last he entered this ring he claimed it was to avenge his family, fallen at the hands of his predecessor."

My eyes snapped to Ahun who was wearing a sly smile. He knew.

"Today he defends his title and rank." The Matron Judge finished.

She turned to face the two fighters again. "I am final judge, should I decide your fight worthy I will announce the winner with the Bone Knife. When I leave the ring you are allowed to fight."

As she backed out the two faced each other. Ahun was taller, and boasted more muscles than the other. Ukzahg was broader, and was trying to hold in a rather impressive mead belly as if he was embarrassed. Once the Matron Judge reached the rope boundary a pair of Orcs lifted the rope and allowed her to cross under without needing to duck. They released the barrier rope once she was clear.

As soon as the rope fell limp Ukzahg barreled into Ahun, trying to knock him into the ground. Ahun took the blow, twisted nimbly, and threw the Challenged to the ground.

Ukzahg growled deeply, spinning around and jumping up to his feet. He charged Ahun again, stopping short from barreling into him and throwing a flurry of punches.

Ahun hunched into a defensive position, putting his hands up to protect his head from the punches.

Suddenly, Ukzahg dropped slightly and threw a punch towards Ahuns' side.

Ahun reacted in kind, grabbing Ukzahg's arm, hyper-extending it, and bringing his other fist into his elbow, shattering and dislocating the joint.

Ukzahg fell to one knee, exclaiming in pain and cradling his injury.

"Do you yield?" Ahun snarled.

"Never." Came the deep response.

Raw anger seeped into Ahuns' features. "You strike Tishna from the books. You lied to me for years, calling me friend, dragging me along after you in your endeavors."

Ahun knelt down in Ukzahgs face. "Did you really think I'd forget?"

Ukzahg blazed, striking Ahun in the head with his own, knocking the High General over. Ukzahg jumped up, kicking Ahun as hard as he could wherever he could.

The iron on my felt colder, heavier, more sinister as I watched my hopes on the ground.

Then Ahun started laughing. He made one, quick movement and Ukzahgs' knee went in the wrong direction with a sickening crack.

The High Chieftain dropped to his side, screaming. Ahun stomped him in the groin a couple times for good measure.

"You've always wanted to overthrow me." Ukzahg gasped. "Give Paryda away, betray her people."

"No." Ahun said, almost a whisper. "I wish to see her grow, and we cannot if we're constantly fighting our neighbors."

Ukzahg tried to stand, but faltered and failed.

Ahun stuck his hand out, near the barrier rope but not crossing the line it made. The Matron Judge handed him the Bone Knife.

Ukzahg tried to shuffle away, fear growing in his eyes.

"I have trained every day since Tishna." He kicked at Ukzahg, hitting him in the ribs. "I have watched and studied you, the traitor." Again he struck out with his heel, hitting the downed Orc in the temple, bouncing his head off the ground.

Ukzahg fell limp into the dirt.

"And you, you grew fat with glutton after you took this title from a man far more worthy." He knelt down at the head of the unconscious Orc. "You send Parydan sons to go and die for you day in and day out. Now, you may join them in the Everswamp, so they may judge your soul for what it's worth."

Ahun paused, glancing up at me. I knew what was to happen. Ukzahg had failed, his life was forfeit. He wanted to make sure I was watching. I didn't want to watch, in my opinion this was murder. Ukzahg was down, he lost. He didn't need to die too.

But all the same I didn't downturn my eyes. For Ahun, I had to watch.

Once he was sure he had my attention he returned his focus to Ukzahg. With one hand he pulled back the other Orcs head, the other positioned the knife to the back of the skull.

In one, swift movement Ahun pushed the dagger through Ukzahgs spinal chord and out the throat.

In that moment, Ahun assumed his throne.

Aelyr instantly started to unlock the chains.

"Thank you." I whispered, feeling a dizzy chill settle over me.

"I wasn't going to let them kill you without a fight." He winked. The half-Elf quickly passed the manacles to the Orc who had brought them over.

The man nodded his thanks as he took them, laying them across his arm like a towel.

The rest of my guards, save Grüdar, swarmed around me, thankful to be back in their place now that the farce was over. Each of them felt the need to squeeze my shoulder or show an extra smile at me. It was warming knowing that they cared, that there were probably just as scared as me in those chains.

We survived, we would all go home safe. The war was over.

All eyes were on Ahun as he stood up, the dripping dagger in his hand. He rose it above his head, glaring at the world around him. "This ends now." He growled, grabbing the flat of the blade with his other hand and snapping the Bone Knife in his hands.

He tossed the two halves on the ground on either side of him and Ukzahg. "For too long we have murdered our ways to power. This needless bloodshed is over. We will find a new way to determine leadership, but this is not the way."

He turned and left the ring.

I wanted to go say congratulations to Ahun, however he was being whisked away by the Matron Judge back into the Hall. Grüdar was behind him, passing over the bearskin robes. He was focused, there was more he had to do, I could speak with him later.

I looked around, suddenly feeling like I had not eaten all week. My stomach was loudly making that point as well. "Soooo... what now?"

The Orc with the manacles chuckled. "Now, we go home. Later, we feast."

We looked at each other, home was quite a while away.

The guard spoke up again. "Worry not, you rested in the Hall, you can return to your rooms."

"Thank you." I said, giving him a slight nod. "And I guess thank you for not killing me when Ukzahg fell."

His smile widened. "I would not have. Few cared for the man."

I looked around at the surroundings, the houses built sparsely between pine trees. The dawn sun shining through the branches casting an almost holy glow on the dispersing crowd. He did not wish me dead. I felt a growing sense of pride in regards to the Orcs, maybe we wouldn't have had to fight for our lives had Ahun fell like we feared.

Aelyr hugged my shoulder, making me wince until he loosened his grip. "Let's go in and see if there's any food left."

I took a deep breath and slowly released it. "Honestly, I could also do with a nap."

Everyone laughed, the tension now gone from the air, as we walked back into the Hall to find food and relax.

TWENTY SEVEN

I didn't see Ahun again until right before dinner when he came to my room. He was wearing a simple tunic and a cape made from another bear pelt, though this one was a single bear. He looked serious, though once he closed the door on the myriad of attendants asking him nonstop questions he relaxed and sagged slightly.

"You doing alright?" I asked.

He went between nodding and shaking his head. "There's just so much to do. Though the gist of everything is that my word is law, no matter what." He took a breath and stared me in the eyes. "That gives me an idea, but I'm not certain the rest of of Asura would approve."

"To hell with them. They stood by knowing that Ukzahg was attacking us and others, they did nothing." I hissed.

Ahun smiled, and proceeded to fill me in with what he had in mind.

* * *

We sat at the table closest to the one where High Chieftan Ahun was seated, the Throne of Paryda standing empty behind him.

Fitz leaned over to me. "Soooo, what now?" He asked with his mouth full.

"Just wait, enjoy the feast." I smiled. We were dressed in some of the finer clothes we had brought with us in hoeps of this very event. While I had left my Collar of Estate at home, I did wear my belt with blade and pistol, each of which stood out rather noticeably.

I knew I heard whispers wondering why Ahun wasn't having me seated with him, I wasn't worried, and I would have turned him down anyway. This was his victory, his time to shine in the spotlight.

The Orcs around us were bustling with enthusiasm and pure joy. I thought the feast last night was impressive, this one laid it to shame. Not only did they have every fire pit in the hall lit and lined with food, large beasts roasting on the rotisseries, but they also brought in braziers featuring pots of stews and vegetables boiling in butter hanging from hooks. The doors and every window were wide open, and every Orc in Hastengrad came in, went before their new High Chieftain to offer well-wishes and tithes, and retiring to one of the tables to partake in the feast laid out before us all.

Only once the crowd coming before him finally faded away, and the boisterous noise of the hall with it, did Ahun rise and speak.

"I have thought long and hard in regards to the future of Paryda." He started. He paused long enough to ensure he had everyone's attention. "Our armies have faced far to many casualties under the rule of Ukzahg. Should any of the countries that my predecessor attacked without due reason should see fit, Paryda would fall despite our best efforts."

He landed a fist on the table, causing a resounding thump. "I will NOT see Paryda fall as I watched my hometown fall. I will not see us stricken from the records of Asura, from the Grand Libraries of the Archipelago, or even from our own lands."

"Then what would you have us do?" Someone asked from the far end of the hall.

"Trust me." Ahun started with. "I will have us join the alliance with Farysha and Bisney. We will have free travel between the countries, but we will still follow most all of our own laws." He took in the shocked faces of the crowd, finally landing his eyes on me. "Lord Bubbles, if you will." He added loud enough for me to hear before walking back to the dais behind him.

I glanced at the guards around me as I slowly stood and joined Ahun by the throne.

"Years ago, when my family fled Paryda during the destruction of Tishna, I joined up with the Faryshan Military and took an oath to serve the Lord, protect the people, and destroy our enemies." He said just loud enough for those in the back to hear him. "Three generations of Faryshan Lords has put me back in my home country."

The High Chieftain of Paryda took a knee before me. "I would swear a new oath this day, should Lord Bubbles permit such, in allegiance to Farysha and her newfound alliance."

I nodded, drawing my sword, my heartbeat thrumming in my ears. Though it made no sound against the leather scabbard, raw power from it sent a thrum through the room. The blade had a rather impressive sub-aura around it, drawn from those who have handled it and those who have been near it, power stored in the inset gems in the crossguard. This was the first time I had drawn the weapon, the raw power of it surprised even me.

The room stood still with silent tension, even the crackling of the fires seemed muted.

I placed the tip of the blade on the ornately embroidered carpet between myself and Ahun. "I permit as such." I said, barely above a whisper, barely able to keep myself from shaking. What can I say, I get bad stagefright.

Though I am certain that the scene looked epic, partly since Ahun kneeling put his eyes just under mine, I felt like a clown pretending to have power. It felt both right and wrong at the same time, but Ahun's cool demeanor helped keep me calm.

He grasped the blade, drawing his own blood from small cuts against the ridge of his palm and pads of his fingers, and brought the tip of the blade to his heart instead.

I was having a hard time staying calm, this was not a part we discussed earlier.

He released his hand, but his gaze locked onto mine, I dared not move the razor sharp sword.

"By my life, by my blood, by my heart, I have and will always serve you, Lord Stan Bubbles of Farysha, soon to be Crown Prince of Bisney, he who leads by love not force, the Golden Dragon of the Faryshan Alliance, until such time you decide that I am no longer fit to reign Paryda or until my death. I will protect the citizens of Paryda, and will not send them into battle needlessly nor against any others who may swear into our Alliance. May the world turn against me, or the swamps swallow me, if I break this solemn oath."

I took a deep breath and removed the blade from Ahun, though I still held it. I hesitated, then drew it against my arm, being careful not to hit a major artery but still draw some blood. The blade thrummed with even more power.

"By my life, by my blood, by my heart I will honor and protect you, High Chieftain Ahun Dragonfist of Paryda. I will not ask anything of you that I would not ask of myself, nor of those under your protection. My the world turn against me, or the dragon fire take me, should I break this solemn oath."

He rose, gesturing for an attendant to clean the blood from the blade. I handed it to the attendant and immediately pulled out the emergency kit I'd been keeping on the back of my belt.

"Give me your hand." I said to Ahun, "Let's see how bad it is."

The cuts weren't overly deep, so I didn't need to stitch anything up thankfully. Just a couple of bandages and Ahun still had full use of his hand. I wrapped my own arm up tight with padding and gauze wrap. I would have to put in stitches once I was no longer shaking. As I was putting my bag back together the attendant returned with the blade.

"Freshly cleaned and oiled, sir." She said.

"Thank you." I took it and slid it back in the scabbard. The tension around it fell silent. "I'll have to talk to Ûlfin about that effect of the sword." I muttered to myself.

Ahun heard the comment. "I agree, I've never seen a sword carry that much power."

"Maybe I should take it to a historian instead." I joked. "I was told that it has been several generations since this sword saw the light of day."

The creases on Ahun's brow deepened as he thought. "I'm betting on six generations past. My predecessor in the Military had served the Lords some time, he said at the start of his career many changes had occurred and the Lord had the Pagoda built."

He shifted to a smile and took a step back. "Anyway, while you are here the throne is yours." He gestured with one hand to the great throne carved from a single tree trunk.

I put my hands up and shook my head. "No, I am an honored guest, I will return to my spot and finish my dinner. Then I'll return to the room I've been staying in."

He bowed slightly. "As you wish then, m'Lord."

I gave him a teasing glare. "You know I don't like it when you call me that."

The smile he returned with was one of pure play and joy. "I know." The smile faded for the most part. "Though before you leave I will need your signature on a few papers to ensure that our oaths pass down to our heirs as necessary."

I almost burst out laughing. "It's been almost a month since I set my eyes on paperwork. It'll be nice to go back to the regular work trying to undo all of what my predecessors fucked up."

"I notice you've been swearing more." Ahun noted, a glint in his eye.

I laughed. "Have you met the men I've spent the last few weeks with? I'm amazed that's the only bad habit I picked up."

We clasped arms at the elbow and pulled each other into a hug. "Let's finish eating and rest. You should probably return to Hykur in the morning before you pick up any more of these bad habits."

I sighed, the smile not leaving my face though the shaking was slowing up. "Yes. I have spent too long away."

He tapped me on the shoulder with a fist. "You also have a wedding to plan for."

I felt my face heat up as I looked away. I was looking forward to spending time with Aleyna. And now that we were finally free from wars I could do so free of worry.

With an awkward smile I returned to my seat and ate in silence, my guards a whirl of cheerful chatter around me. The Orcs in the hall seemed to agree with Ahun's choices, not a one looked to be upset with their new High Chieftain.

My group was of the first to retire. We said our good nights to Ahun before returning to our rooms. He tried to convince us to move over to his side of the Hall, but we chose not to. We had already settled in where we were at, and if we already were leaving in the morning we didn't want to pack up our bags twice.

As my guards and the rest of the soldiers who had come with us retired to their rooms, I went to the bathroom sink and began cutting off the wrappings. Focusing my aura on my arm to numb the pain and slow up the bloodflow as I worked.

While I could stitch up a cut in record time, that was always on someone else. It was awkward trying to sew up my own left arm. After a few minutes I was stitched up, and I wrapped the cut up to prevent the injury from re-opening and getting infected.

Once that was finished I packed my kit back up, taking note of what I needed to replace from use, and returned to my room. Despire how sore I was I felt odd, like I was as light as a feather. We won. I now ran an alliance of three countries. Ahun had called me The Golden Dragon. One month ago I was just a doctor, working to save lives as they came to me. Now, I was far more. Not only did I still try to save all I could, but even more lives depended on me to make the right decisions.

My soldiers especially. The children who fought for me.

I shook my head, trying to clear my thoughts as I pulled on my pajamas and climbed into bed.

Sleep came easier to me then than it had since I took up my mantle. Though my dreams were still the faces of the men I couldn't save. The children who died before me. Who died for me.

I swore I would not forget them, ever. Something had to change to keep more from an early death if anything else were to happen.

TWENTY EIGHT

I was led to Ahun's office by a young maiden. The door was open and he was busy throwing boxes out of the door.

"What is it with leadership and sex?" He yelled, a growl in his voice.

Another box hit the wall and broke open, revealing quite a few items that really should not be in a professional setting.

More voices came from the room, all female, though I could not understand them.

"Look," Ahun said over them, "I know Ukzahg was your owner, but I'm getting rid of all types of slavery. Go, live your own lives and for the love of all the Gods STOP TRYING TO PULL OFF MY PANTS EVERY TIME I WALK IN HERE!"

"Maybe this is a bad time...?" Aelyr asked, tapping my shoulder.

I chuckled. "Sounds like he's having a worse time than I had."

Cautiously, I walked up to the room and peeked in through the door. Ahun towered over a series of scantily clad Orc women. I dare say that his already red complexion was even brighter red than normal.

Smiling, I knocked on the doorframe, causing the girls to jump and turn. "Bad time?" I asked.

The girls allowed Ahun to usher them out and down the hallway, a few of them bending to pick up a box, and each of them making that simple act look amazing.

Once they were gone we entered the room, depositing our bags near the door.

"The transport is ready for you by the front doors." Ahun said, sifting through the papers on his desk. "Let's get these signed. I'll have to get you the paperwork on who is taking over the High General position later." His eyes tracked to the door. "I've had a handful trying to keep them off me whenever I'm alone."

"I'm suddenly glad that the only issue I had to deal with was the amount of porn." I chuckled, scratching the back of my head.

The look he shot me was that of pure and sudden jealousy. I also noted that it looked like he hadn't slept the night before, heavy bags were under his eyes, and he carried himself with more weariness than normal.

"Everything alright, Ahun?" I asked, suddenly worried.

"They didn't let me sleep last night." He focused back on the desk, setting some papers aside and others in a small stack.

"The girls?"

He paused, not looking at me, his hands frozen in the air. "Not just them." He whispered. "Then again, the rest are nothing new, I have grown used to them. So yes, the girls."

Ahun put one more piece on the stack and stepped back. "These, please. Should be obvious where to sign."

I walked up to the desk which looked higher than mine. Then again, Orcs are taller than Humans too, so that wasn't surprising. "Do they need an official seal too?"

"No, just your signature will do."

I nodded and steadily signed the pieces of paper right over where my name was typed out formally. The process only took a couple minutes before I straightened and stretched.

Ahun glanced over them before nodding. "Looks good."

I glanced back out the door. "You going to be alright out here?"

He smiled. "I can handle some girls that just got too used to something." The smile faded. "Though they never should have been put in that situation to begin with. I'll have to keep a close eye on them to make sure they don't go into whoring themselves out and get sick."

"How did my family ever end up with such good men?" I shook my head in amazement.

He smirked and let out a chuckle. "We joined up for the tax break. We stayed in hoping to help nullify the evil from your predecessors." He looked away. "If you're worried about your men, look at the Guard. They're the enforcers of the laws. If anyone will have issues with you decreasing their workload, they'll be there."

It hurt to think of Ûlfin being in charge of such atrocities, of having done some of them himself as he climbed the ranks. Maybe that was why he is such a good man now.

Or is he?

Suddenly the doubts entered my mind and wouldn't leave. Could Ûlfin be trusted?

Ahun seemed to read my mind, or at least the sudden worry and confusion apparent on my face. "Don't worry." He said. "We have all done things we didn't like, you included. I trust the man, he has done more to keep the Lords from killing everyone in Farysha more times than I can count. He has also kept the borders safe for just as long."

I snorted. "Unless it's riot season."

Ahun gave me a stern look. "He was always told to step down when the Lord incited riots. He hates doing so."

"Is that why no one told me of the riots that occurred when I stepped up?"

He sighed deeply. "Ûlfin led a team to stop the riots before they began in earnest. I'm sure you noticed that he had become abnormally tired."

I hadn't. I had been too focused on my work. I didn't see what Ûlfin had been doing to make sure Hykur and Farysha were safe for our guests, much less myself.

I looked away, ashamed.

Ahun placed a hand on my shoulder. "Don't be hard on yourself, it's been a busy month."

I nodded. I knew he was right, but I couldn't bring myself to speak. Things were so much easier just over a month ago, when all I had to worry about was avoiding Harry and the rest of my family. It still hurt, I still had to fight to keep the tears from coming. Some pain will never truly go away.

The fingers on my shoulder tightened in compassion. "Go home, Stan." Ahun almost whispered. "Go rest, you've earned it."

"So have you." I responded, my voice barely audible.

He smiled sadly. "My work has just begun. Soon enough, yes, I will take some time to kick back and relax. For now, though, there's much to be done."

"Still much in Farysha as well."

"Ah, the curse of those in charge, the work that never ends."

I smiled slightly, the humor helping but only just.

Ahun removed his hand and went behind his desk, shuffling more of the papers and coughing slightly at a cloud of dust. "Until we meet again, m'Lord."

"Until we meet again, Lord Ahun." I bowed my head in respect.

We shared one more, brief, smile before I turned and grabbed my bags, my guards bidding Ahun farewell and following me out as well.

The plan was to leave from here and stay two nights at the encampment we stayed at on the way here to allow us to back the rest of our gear. From there we were to head back to Hykur.

The ride to camp was quiet. Even Kutz was quiet. Everyone looked weary, even with the feast and a good nights sleep. It was the stress of the past month. War, fighting to Hastengrad. Standing there, helpless, as Ahun fought Ukzahg, knowing that we were all dead should he fail. While we were relieved, we knew there were going to be repercussions for what just happened. Many would see the fight as an assassination, especially now that Paryda was also under my control instead of being its' sole country attacking others as the High Chieftain saw fit.

Lord of the Faryshan Alliance. It felt odd. I didn't even want to rule one country, and now I have two. Gods, at some point in the future I would rule Bisney as well as King.

I felt sick to my stomach. It was too much. I didn't want any of it.

But I wouldn't be alone.

That night, back in my cot, having packed my bags save for the clothes I was going to ride home in, I dreamt of Aleyna and our future together.

TWENTY NINE

That next day we woke early and loaded back into the transport. We were told that there were soldiers who were going to dismantle the tent for us, so we didn't have to worry.

This time Kutz and others picked back up in song. We drove alone, no caravan to join us. Ahun had Colonel Helesia steadily move a camp back, a days travel, so those traveling to and from Hastengrad had a place to rest and refuel.

Thankfully there were few soldiers who had been injured so as to still need beds in Recovery, mostly accidents around camp, so that is where we spent the night.

We left again early in the morning with well wishes from Helesia and Captian Fíla.

Again the guards took up song, some even tried to dance in the back of the transport, falling over and almost hurting themselves whenever we hit a bump. That made us all laugh until our sides hurt, or hurt more, depending on who you were talking about.

Before we knew it night was falling, and we were finally back in Farysha. We stopped in a small town near the border, just out of the mountain range, to stretch our legs and eat something. I left anything that denoted me as the Lord in the transport, but as we still looked like soldiers we were given a small amount of reverence.

We ate the greasiest, most unhealthy food we could find. For once, I didn't care. We all ate with gusto, having spent the last few days eating R.E.M.s. The food wasn't as good as the Orcish feast, but it was still pretty damn good.

It was nearing midnight when we finally reached Hykur and the Red Pagoda. As soon as we stepped inside, looking ready to fall over, assistants ran over to carry our bags for us.

For once, I let them.

I barely remember the ride up the elevator, mostly Kutz almost drunkinly blurting out whatever offtune song he could think of to cover the godawful music that could never be changed.

The Penthouse was empty, most of the staff having gone home or to their rooms for the night. Ûlfin, Brock, and Aleyna stood there, each looking like they had just been woken from a deep slumber. Aleyna was holding Sir Snowball who wriggled free when he saw me and ran over, purring loudly.

I picked up the furball and hugged him close. "Missed you too buddy."

Brock chuckled as we walked over. "What of the rest of us?"

I smiled down at him. "Naaahhhhhhh, you mean more paperwork." I drew out the word sarcastically. I paused and burst out laughing. "I did, all three of you."

Ûlfin smirked down at me. "Good, cause we didn't miss you changing all the terrible laws nonstop and giving us less work to do."

Aleyna gave the Orc a slight tap that was probably meant to be a punch. "Says ze man that took two weeks vacation and came back whining zat Stan wasn't here to take up the workload."

He smiled warmly at her. "It is called a joke, m'Lady."

She stifled a yawn. "I guess I'm too tired to think clearly."

"Then let's all go to bed." I suggested.

Sir Snowball jumped from my arms as the Princess came over and wrapped me in a tight hug. I hugged her back. It felt nice.

"Welcome home, Stan." She said. "I did miss your company whilst you were away."

"And me, you. More than I expected."

She broke the hug and smiled up at me. She yawned in full, so I put my arm around her shoulders.

"Let's all go to bed."

She nodded and walked off towards the stairs, she was still staying in a bedroom on the upper floor.

My cat followed me to my bed, the guards went their separate ways, all of them too tired to stay up and stand guard. Tonight, and possibly tomorrow, they would rely on the guards downstairs to do their job.

I disrobed, changed into my pajamas, and collapsed into bed. I don't remember falling asleep, or any dreams. I just remember my face hitting the pillow, then waking up on top of my sheets.

I rolled over, it didn't feel like I had slept at all, though I did feel slightly more awake than I had that night.

Grabbing a blanket and tossing it over my shoulders I left my room, wincing at the brightness of the hallway. Aelyr and Kutz stood outside, obviously tired.

"How are you two awake?" I asked.

"Coffee. Magic." Kutz said, apparently only capable of single word sentences.

I nodded. "Coffee sounds good."

Together we stumbled down the hall and all but collapsed into the closest chairs we could find at the table.

Ûlfin came over at some point, we had been staring blankly at the table, the waiters couldn't even snap us out of the tired trance. Kutz had already passed out against the table, snoring loudly.

The Orc shook his head as he looked us over. He grabbed a waiter, asking to bring us something simple and small.

I blinked and my head was against the table, small rolls with bowls of jams in front of my face. Ûlfin was sitting further down the table, eating on a similar fare with the addition of a large platter of bacon.

Slowly Aelyr and I nibbled on the rolls. Only once we were done did Kutz wake up and partake as well, and did Ûlfin walk over.

"Go back to bed." He said, resting a hand on my shoulder. I didn't look at him, I was just too tired.

"Need work." I responded, reverting to single word sentences myself. He chuckled. "No, you need rest. We can bring you food to your bed when you wake up, but you won't be making good choices like this." I nodded, though that might have been me more nodding off where I sat. Ûlfin helped me up, and steadied me as he led me back to my room, being careful to avoid the wrap around my arm.

I managed to crawl back under the covers and was shortly back asleep. This time dreams came to me. Again I saw the faces of the young men, I felt the terror as I tried to save them, knowing I couldn't. They came again and again. I remembered what I did wrong each time, rectifying the mistakes, using more magic, more power, anything I could possibly do.

Each time I felt their aura fade under my hands. I watched their confused eyes glaze over as death came for them. Felt each tear roll down my face as I had to turn from them to yet another to die beneath my hands. Suddenly it wasn't just the children from the fighting. Others I couldn't save over the past decade came before me, asking me why I couldn't save them. Why I didn't.

I tried to answer, but my mouth had been stitched shut. I could see anger enter into their dead eyes. Fear entered my heart as they sat up and came closer.

I woke up in a cold sweat in the middle of the day. Sir Snowball was tight against my chest, purring as he watched me. I pet his head for a moment before he pounced off, scratching at the door to be let out.

One of the guards outside, I was assuming Fits and Hans, let him out and glanced in. I couldn't tell who it was from the silhouette back-lit by the harsher lights as he looked in.

I over-exaggerated rolling over, pulling my comforter up over my shoulders even moreso than it was. I didn't want to talk to anyone at the moment. Nor was I hungry enough to get up and eat.

I couldn't get the images of all the death out of my head. I knew they weren't children, but they were still almost twenty years younger than me. I knew they chose to join the military, they knew the risks.

But it was a war that wasn't needed, pushed on us by a madman trying to kill me. Had the assassin succeeded this wouldn't have happened.

Something felt, different. I felt like I should be curled up, crying myself to sleep as I had been doing my first week in office. But I wasn't. Instead I was staring into the distance blankly.

I felt empty. Beyond empty. It was cold, despite my blanket and heavy comforter.

I noticed I was shaking, but I wasn't cold even though I felt a certain chill. I knew something was wrong, and I wasn't sure which.

I froze when I heard the door open slightly and soft footsteps walked in. It was Aleyna.

Without a word she came in behind me, staying on top of the sheets, and placing her arm around my shoulder.

The shivering stopped. Her embrace was warm, it felt nice.

We lay there in silence. We didn't speak. There was no need. She understood that there were things I just saw, just went through. Patients that I was not emotionally attached to, save for the attempt to save their lives, was far different than men who were getting injuries and facing death because of me. For me. All in a war I did not desire, that I did not ask for. A young man that was hit by a bus I didn't know, it made my job easier. The young man with half his face blown off who carried my colors on his shoulder.... He was my soldier. His life and death was on my shoulders, and no one else's.

I couldn't remember the number of deaths, the amount of funeral pyres I attended. The number of young men who risked and lost their lives because of me.

She had only lost a fraction of the lives I just had. Every soldier was a part of my family in my mind. We lost over a hundred in merely a month.

I didn't realize when I had fallen asleep, but this time I woke refreshed and relaxed.

Still, I didn't want to leave my bed.

Slowly I stood, but only because my stomach was making me.

Brock met me for breakfast. He told me there were letters than had come in for me that needed my attention when I was feeling up to it, but I shouldn't keep them waiting for too long.

I was planning on taking the day off anyway, and dealing with paperwork again tomorrow.

Aleyna came down and sat besides me.

"Feeling any better?"

I nodded. "A little, thank you."

We both smiled, hers was a little wider than mine. I didn't have to completely force mine, just a little forcing.

"It must be hard." She said, looking at the plate brought over for her. "You know I will always be here if you need to talk about it."

"I will, in time." I wasn't touching my plate, despite the complaining of my stomach. "They were children, Aleyna, all of them. I couldn't save them, send them home to their parents." My held my fork in a white knuckled grip.

She placed her hand on mine. "Zey were adults, Stan. In time you will come to see. You can't blame yourself."

I took a shaky breath. "But, in a way, it was. I know it was Ukzahg who started the war, but had I died instead at the hands of his assassin child...." I clenched my jaw and looked away.

"Had you died instead the he would have invaded Farysha looking to expand his borders. Many more would have died without leadership."

I shook my head. "Ûlfin and Ahun would have been able to lead the armies to success. He knew that. He would have backed down."

Her grip on my hand tightened. "But zere's no way we can know zat for certain. Besides, it is in the past now. Let us remember ze honored dead, not focus on zem so much zat zeir souls remain trapped here."

She did have a point. I relaxed, and her smile grew more relaxed.

"Zere." She said. "Now eat something, Zat will help you feel better."

We ate in silence, though it wasn't as tense as it had been before. Brock excused himself, adding that Her Highness was right, that I'm beating myself up over something that was unavoidable.

She was right, I felt better after getting a full meal in my stomach. She rose from the table first, leaving her plate. I gathered it and my own and brought it into the kitchens, taking the time to wash them and set them aside to dry. I didn't want to forget who I had been, the more simple me, the Doctor.

Once the small task was finished I found Aleyna standing on the balcony, looking out at Hykur.

"Farysha is lovely, don't you think?" She asked.

I looked out at the scene. Hykur glowed under the golden rays of the sun. Parts glistened, apparently it had rained the day before. The Sleeping Volcano stood dark against the blue sky deep in the distance. Then I looked at her. Her sandy hair was loose, swaying in the gentle breeze, taking on a golden sheen. Her unique eyes bright and cheerful, taking in the scene before her. She looked young, but was beautiful all the same. I found a sense of pride inside me, a feeling that I truly did enjoy her, more than just for the political alliance.

"Yea, it's wonderful." I said, not taking my eyes off her.

She looked over at me and blushed. The act made me smile earnestly for the first time since I got back home, since the reality of the past few weeks sunk into me.

Impulse took over me. Gently I took her hand and pulled her into a kiss.

Her lips felt warm and lovely against mine, as we embraced in the glow of the city. She leaned into it, a hint of desire in her actions.

She was soft, warm, and her aura blushed with a wave of activity. It had been over a decade since I felt the touch of a woman in such a way. I felt a slight moan escape my throat, a sound which she matched.

I ran a shuddering hand through her hair, feeling her hand run to the small of my back.

We stood like that a moment before breaking our embrace, breathlessly looking at each other. I smiled and rested my forehead against hers, closing my eyes and just enjoying the sensation of her against me.

"We can get through this." I whispered, "Together, we can do this."

She hugged me tight, I hugged her back. I didn't realize how much I needed that small touch of comfort. "Yes, we can."

About the Author

Kim Adkins is a new author who loves to merge traditional fantasy with science fiction. This love for the mix came about as she tested genres in high school and college alongside different art techiques and mediums. When she isn't writing, she's working on reproducing historical designs on painted glass, or is out practicing expirimental archeology with living history groups.

Milton Keynes UK
Ingram Content Group UK Ltd.
UKHW020632100424
440866UK00015B/384